La detective
está muerta.

The
Detective
Is Already
Dead

nigozyu
Illustration by Umibouzu

Danny Bryant

— Kimihiko's "teacher"

"What're you standing there and spacing out for? Starting today, this is your home."

"I mean, even if you suddenly tell me to live here..."

Kimihiko Kimizuka

—Grade schooler

Cosplay
Ace Detective

"You're a
guardian of
the world.
Get it
together,
would you?"

"B-boss?
What are you wearing...?"

Siesta

I was lazing around on the bed,
holding the phone up high, when Mia
started panicking. Come to think of it,
I was still in my underwear.

《Tuners》 | A group of twelve messengers who exist to preserve the world's stability and harmony. Each has their own position and mission, and they're constantly fighting the crises that assail the world. If a Tuner ███, a replacement is appointed directly by the Federation Government. At such times, a new position may be established as well.

《Global Crisis/ Enemies》 | A collective term for wars, environmental destruction, and other man-made global crises, as well as historically or scientifically unforeseen hostile phenomena or entities. Examples include World War III, the Primordial Seed (see below), and the Rebellion of ███

《The Primordial Seed》 | A global crisis that first invaded Earth fifty years ago. The enemy of the Ace Detective, one of the Tuners. It disguised itself as a human, used its own clones to form an organization known as SPES, and worked to ensure that its seeds would thrive on Earth. During its final battle, it used up its strength and was absorbed into Yggdrasil. However, it left its ███ on this planet.

《The Sacred Text》 | Volumes that foretell global crises. Compiled by the Oracle, one of the Tuners. Their content is top secret: As a rule, even high-ranking Federation Government officials aren't allowed to read them. ███ stole part of them, but due to the criminal's peculiar trait, it isn't clear what was stolen. The matter is currently under investigation.

《The Federation Government》 | An organization known as the world's government, centered around the Mizoev Federation. Its greatest objective is to protect the world from crises, and it transcends the frameworks of nations and continents. They are all ███ already, and they rarely show themselves in public.

《The Federal Charter》 | Rules and agreements imposed on the Tuners regarding the Federal Council in which they participate. Except for ███ ███, and others like them, almost no one knows who, when, or how they created the Federal Charter.

《The Akashic Records》 | One of the world's secrets, and the reason behind World War III. They're said to be the plans for a biological weapon that could destroy the world, or classified political information that all the countries of the world have consigned to oblivion; however, there's no need for mankind to know what they actually are.
　　With the help of the Tuners, the Mizoev Federation's policy prevented World War III from causing any real damage, and kept the Akashic records from being leaked. The world will continue to enjoy lasting peace.

《The Singularity》 | In order to maintain a peaceful world, it would be best to ███ as soon as possible.

The Detective Is Already Dead

6

nigozyu

Illustration by Umibouzu

YEN
ON

New York

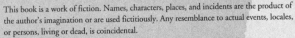

The Detective Is Already Dead, Vol. 6

nigozyu

Translation by Taylor Engel

Cover art by Umibouzu

TANTEI HA MO SHINDEIRU, Vol.6
©nigozyu 2021
First published in Japan in 2021 by KADOKAWA CORPORATION, Tokyo.
English translation rights arranged with KADOKAWA CORPORATION, Tokyo, through TUTTLE-MORI AGENCY, INC., Tokyo.

English translation © 2023 by Yen Press, LLC

Yen On
150 West 30th Street, 19th Floor
New York, NY 10001

Visit us at yenpress.com
facebook.com/yenpress
twitter.com/yenpress
yenpress.tumblr.com
instagram.com/yenpress

First Yen On Edition: August 2023
Edited by Yen On Editorial: Shella Wu, Anna Powers
Designed by Yen Press Design: Andy Swist

Yen On is an imprint of Yen Press, LLC.
The Yen On name and logo are trademarks of Yen Press, LLC.

Library of Congress Cataloging-in-Publication Data
Names: nigozyu, author. | Umibouzu, illustrator. | Engel, Taylor, translator.
Title: The detective is already dead / nigozyu ; illustration by Umibouzu ; translation by Taylor Engel.
Other titles: Tantei wa Mou, Shindeiru. English
Description: First Yen On edition. | New York, NY : Yen On, 2021.
Identifiers: LCCN 2021012132 | ISBN 9781975325756 (v. 1 ; trade paperback); ISBN 9781975325770 (v. 2 ; trade paperback); ISBN 9781975325794 (v. 3 ; trade paperback); ISBN 9781975348250 (v. 4 ; trade paperback); ISBN 9781975360122 (v. 5 ; trade paperback); ISBN 9781975368975 (v. 6 ; trade paperback)
Subjects: GSAFD: Mystery fiction.
Classification: LCC PL873.5.I46 T3613 2021 | DDC 895.63/6—dc23
LC record available at https://lccn.loc.gov/2021012132

ISBNs: 978-1-9753-6897-5 (paperback)
978-1-9753-6898-2 (ebook)

10 9 8 7 6 5 4 3 2 1

LSC-C

Printed in the United States of America

The Detective Is Already Dead

6

Contents

7 years ago, Kimihiko

"So you're pleading 'not guilty' again this time?"

I was at my regular police station, watching an officer with grizzled hair organize his report. He was wearing a grim smile. Even I thought I probably looked exhausted.

"Like I said, I didn't do it." Seriously, what fifth grader would snatch a bag from a random lady on the street?

"Hmm. I wouldn't put it past you, though."

"You're overestimating me, mister."

Wait, should that have been "underestimating"? I heaved a big sigh. This police station felt as comforting to me as my own home.

Do people become "regulars" at police stations, you ask? They do if they're me. As a matter of fact, this is the third time this week that I've met this officer (who's apparently in charge around here). That's more times than I've been to school.

What? I'm skipping too much for a grade schooler? Well, what am I supposed to do? Say I see an old lady with a cane trying to get across a crosswalk while I'm on my way to school. I help her, and then I find out that she's a victim of a bank transfer scam. Before you know it, I've been pulled into a scuffle with an enormous organized fraud ring. I've had a knack for getting dragged into trouble since I was born, and that's just how it is. There was no time to sit around in school.

Today, for example, I'd been caught up in a bag-snatching incident on my way to class, then was suspected of perpetrating it. Now here I was, fighting a pointless battle at the police station with its chief.

"You had nothing on me yesterday, you've got nothing today, and you won't have anything on me tomorrow, either. I mean, I'm innocent."

"Not guilty" sometimes carries a different nuance. It's the term they use when they can't charge you with a crime due to insanity or lack of evidence. In my case, though, I really didn't snatch that bag, nor was I involved with the bank transfer scam. I'm not just "not guilty," I straight up didn't do it. I remember checking in a dictionary when I was bored in Modern Japanese class once.

"You sure know a lot for a kid your age," the chief drawled. Even then, he kept scrutinizing my face. "I'm almost at retirement age, see. I was planning to take it easy at a police station for my last few years on duty, but thanks to you, I'm busier than I've ever been in my whole career. ...Granted, I haven't been bored," he added with a grin.

If he's close to retiring, is somebody else going to be in charge of this police station someday? Since I can't change this annoying predisposition of mine, I'm definitely going to keep ending up here. Here's hoping that the next guy is more laidback.

"Can I go home? You must know by now that I didn't do anything."

A surveillance camera near the crime scene had caught a man who seemed to be the fleeing bag-snatcher. Our heights were totally different, so I'd been told I was off the suspect list. Saved by my youth, although I hope I get taller eventually.

"Besides, I've got a curfew." I got up from the metal folding chair.

I didn't mean I had a strict dad and mom waiting for me at home. What was waiting for me were *the facility's rules*. I couldn't remember ever having a family. I was an orphan. As far as I was concerned, just having a place that guaranteed my right to live was a great thing.

"Hang out just a little longer. I hear they're sending someone to pick you up today," the chief said.

Someone to pick me up? What was that about? Ever since the woman who was in charge of the children's home picked up on this knack of mine, for better or worse, she acted like any trouble I caused wasn't her problem. I really couldn't see her coming to a police station to pick me up...

"See? Speak of the devil." The director's eyes focused on something behind me. "He's your guarantor. So even you have family, huh?"

That made me turn around.

A middle-aged man in a suit was standing there, a top hat pulled down low over his eyes. He looked well-dressed at first, but on closer inspection, his suit and shirt were shabby, and his worn-out leather shoes had mud on them. His eyes were shadowed, but they were sharp as an animal's.

"Who are you?" I asked.

With a big, wolfish grin, the man introduced himself.

"—Danny. Danny Bryant."

That was how I met my "teacher."

Danny took me to a run-down apartment building that had to be forty years old. After you came through the front door, a second interior door opened into a traditional Japanese-style room that was about thirteen square meters. I shouldn't have been familiar with the scent of tatami, but it struck me as weirdly nostalgic. Maybe that just came with being Japanese.

"What are you standing there and spacing out for?" the man asked behind me. As he walked past me, he said, "Starting today, this is your home." Then he plopped down on the floor in front of the low table.

Right off the bat, he opened a can of beer. He'd picked it up at a convenience store on our way back from the police station.

"I mean, even if you suddenly tell me to live here..." Bewildered, I looked around. The walls were decorated with strange items that seemed to be souvenirs from overseas, and antiques and pieces of fine art were littered here and there around the room.

Was he into traveling, or was he a hoarder? The idea of living here with this total stranger was starting to make my head hurt.

"Ha-ha. Don't overthink it, grade-schooler," the man said, calling me by a random title. Or maybe it was more of a category. "Don't get attached to ideas like 'home' or 'places to belong.' You're in elementary school, so just think of it as...a secret base here. Yeah. That's true for me, too," Danny added.

Apparently, he had several places, and this apartment was just one of them. Judging from all the souvenirs lying around, it looked like he really did spend most of his time traveling.

"Then you're not always going to be here?" I pulled a floor cushion over and sat down a little ways from him.

"That's right. Don't expect me to take care of you, got it?"

"...So first you introduce yourself as family, and then you say that?" Was this any better than the strict group living situation at the facility?

"Well, if you insist. I'll pay the rent, the electricity bill, and the water bill. I am the adult here, after all."

"That's not a very mature way to put it. ...What about living expenses?"

"You're going to earn those yourself. Oh, I'm not telling you to go get a job. I'll bring work home, and you'll help me out with it. It'll be compensation," Danny said, knocking back his beer.

"...I'm still in grade school, remember?"

"In this world, there are tons of eleven-year-olds who work. Don't assume your common sense is gonna be normal everywhere."

You talk like you've seen it. I almost said it aloud, sarcastically, then realized he actually might have. What had this guy seen in his travels around the globe?

"Let's set some house rules."

As if the man had just read my mind, he made a proposal:

"While we're both using this as a home base, let's not pry into each other's affairs."

Saying that was the only rule, Danny told me to promise. He looked serious.

"If it's important enough to be your only rule, I'm guessing you have some sort of *secret* you really don't want strangers to know?"

"Ha-ha! You're sharp, kid!" The man laughed off my amateur deduction like it was straight out of a comedy movie.

We'd only met half an hour ago, but my first impression of him had been that he was going to be tiring to be around. He had yet to prove me wrong.

"There's one more thing I want to ask." He'd just made me promise not to pry, but he was the one who dragged me here today unwarranted. I should be allowed at least one more question, so I asked: "Why did you take me in?"

He'd said he was family, but that had to be a lie. In this instance, what benefit was there in taking me in?

No, if he'd been after physical labor, there were better candidates out there. Was he just helping a kid who'd drawn a bad lot in life? Since the police had acknowledged him, was this a legal, legitimate foster arrangement? But nobody had said anything about it to me...

"You always look for the reasons behind everything. You're a smart kid." The man gazed at me and narrowed his eyes. And then: "Remember that mindset, and someday, try to solve that mystery."

He grinned, flashing his white teeth. In the end, he never answered my question.

"Sorry. It's an adults-only sort of thing."

"...That's my least favorite phrase ever."

"Ha-ha! I see. Then as an apology, we'll get whatever you want for dinner. What sounds good?" The man crushed his empty beer can in his hand and reached for another one.

Something occurred to me as I watched him. "I always wanted to order a pizza," I said.

When I told him to make it a large, the man said, "I figured you'd say that, so I ordered it already. It'll be here in five." He laughed, cell phone in hand.

That was how my strange life with Danny began.

A certain boy's tale 1

Singapore: a hot, humid country where it feels like summer all year round. Right now, the four of us were in one of its commuter towns.

"My, that looks delicious!"

We were sitting in an eatery that faced the street, and a pleasant wind was blowing through. Across from me, Saikawa energetically clapped her hands together over her lunch. "Thanks for the food!"

From what I heard, it had won a star in a world-famous restaurant guidebook, but it was in a place resembling a food court on the first floor of an apartment building. Apparently, that was really common here. It reminded me how different cultures could be.

"Haaaah. Lunch. Finally." Charlie shot me a cranky look across the table. "It's incredible how just having a certain someone around can ruin our plans."

Grumbling about how it was a total nuisance, she started slurping her pork noodles.

She seemed to have a problem with the fact that I'd accidentally caught a *pickpocket* on our way to the eatery, and dealing with it had taken up time.

"Easy, easy. We're still ahead of schedule. No harm done." From the seat next to mine, Natsunagi tried to calm Charlie down. She was smiling a bit awkwardly.

The reason we'd come to Singapore was because of a conference with high-ranking officials from the Federation Government that was scheduled to take place at six o'clock that evening. There, they would address Nagisa Natsunagi's appointment as a Tuner. They were going to hand down a formal decision about whether it was appropriate to make her the new Ace Detective.

"It could end up being a tough debate. Let's recharge while we've got the chance." Telling myself that as much as the rest of them, I stabbed a big piece of chicken with my fork.

"The Ace Detective, huh...?" Natsunagi gazed into the distance. She was probably mulling over the many nuances of that title. If a new Ace Detective was being appointed, it meant that someone else had stepped down from the position.

The name of that person was Siesta.

A month ago, Siesta had retaken her heart and joined our final battle against Seed, the world's enemy. Ultimately, through the sacrifice of our former enemy Hel, Seed had been sealed within an enormous tree, and our long story had come to an end. —Or it should have, anyway.

After that fight, *certain circumstances* had forced Siesta to fall asleep, and she'd been asleep ever since. Even now, she was in Japan, napping. We'd decided not to bring the curtain down on this tale until we found a way to wake her up.

"We're just getting started, aren't we?" Next to me, Natsunagi slapped her cheeks with her hands, psyching herself up.

True, there were things that we'd lost, and things that had changed. But we'd managed to hold on to a few things, too.

"Kimizuka? Is something wrong?" Natsunagi tilted her head, looking puzzled. The wind blew, ruffling her hair softly. She had cut her hair short.

I felt as if I'd caught a glimpse of her other face, the one that had once lived inside her.

"Nah, I was just thinking beautiful girls look great with any haircut."

"...Have you always been the type to say things like that without blushing, Kimizuka?" she asked in a small, weak voice.

"I figured out that everything goes more smoothly when I'm honest."

The former Ace Detective was the one who taught me that pacing was important. Anybody could see that exacerbating problems by saying things I didn't actually think, or not saying what I did think, would just make people hate me. Most of all, it wouldn't help anyone who was involved. I'd learned as much over the past several months, through several various incidents.

"In that case, Kimizuka, compliment me, too!" Saikawa said, raising her hand and butting into our conversation.

"I don't get what 'in that case' means here."

"Oh, come on, Kimizuka. Idols are constantly hungry for approval."

"They shouldn't say things like that with a straight face."

Well, never mind. Pacing matters here, too.

Gazing steadily across the table at Saikawa, I complimented her on everything I could think of: the nails she'd clearly put a ton of work into, the hairstyle she'd tried out for the first time, her new shampoo, and the scent of her perfume.

"...Oh, yes, I see. U-um, thank you very much..."

"Hey, Saikawa. Why did your face tense up? And why did you scoot your chair back a bit?"

That's weird. I complimented her because she told me to. This is way too unf—

"No, getting turned off by that is completely appropriate," Natsunagi said with a look of disgust before I could give my usual sigh. "That's just freaky. A girl gets scared when you're paying that close attention."

"But a detective's assistant has to be able to observe people, right?"

"We're telling you not to do that with girls!"

Natsunagi and Saikawa clung to each other, saying "That's really scary," and shooting me cold looks.

What did I do to deserve this treatment, huh?

"Sheesh. Charlie, it looks like it's two against two here."

"Why are you assuming I'm on your side, Kimizuka?"

Even the blond agent, the member of this group I'd known the longest, stared at me in disgust.

"You know, Charlie, your birthday's coming up. Is there anything you want?"

"And now you're trying to win me over with presents?! ...Actually, why do you know when my birthday is, Kimizuka?"

It didn't really mean anything. I was partnered with a detective who was really big on celebrating anniversaries, that's all.

"K-Kimizuka actually knows when my birthday is... Wait, why am I kind of happy about that? It's such a stupid little..."

"Yui! Quit doing stupid voice-overs for me!" Using her hands, Charlie messed up Saikawa's hair.

"Sorry~~," Saikawa said, but she was wearing a joyful smile.

I bet watching a peaceful scene like this when you're eating makes it taste 20 percent better.

"You didn't give me a present." Ignoring the two of them, Natsunagi looked at me as if to say something more.

If I recalled, her birthday was—June 7.

That had been right before she and I met in that classroom after school, and she'd asked me to find the original owner of her heart.

"Yours will have to wait until next year."

"You mean we'll be together next year, too?" For some reason, Natsunagi seemed happy. She tucked her hair behind her ears.

Next year. If all went well, we would have graduated high school by then. What would our lives be like? Would all our wishes have come true?

"Mine is in December, so you have plenty of time!" Saikawa, who'd apparently been eavesdropping, announced in hope for a birthday present next.

"Do you even have anything else you want, Saikawa?"

Just looking at her mansion, you'd figure she already had everything.

"That may be true for physical things, but in exchange, there's, um, something I want to do…" Uncharacteristically, she faltered. Then she glanced up at us. "I'd like to have a birthday party with all of you."

Saikawa hadn't grown up taking that sort of thing for granted, and she said her wish timidly.

"We'll do it! We're absolutely having one!" Jumping up with a clatter, Natsunagi reached across the table and hugged Saikawa.

For a moment, Saikawa seemed startled, then relieved.

One thing had led to another and another and another, but through it all, Natsunagi and Saikawa had become fast friends as well.

"You don't need in on that?"

The awkward blond girl was watching those two from up close, and she kept putting out her hand, hesitating, then retracting it. She didn't seem to have the courage to jump into that circle just yet.

"I'm fine," Charlie murmured softly, as if she'd given up. Even so, she took out a notebook and started to write something into her schedule for some future date.

"…What?"

Oh, nothing. I just thought *She sure isn't honest, huh.* She's a lot like I used to be.

"Come to think of it, has your birthday passed already, Kimizuka? I would have wanted to celebrate that as well," Saikawa said.

"Kimizuka's is May fifth."

"Charlie, why did you answer that?"

And, what, you know my birthday?

"Huh. That's Children's Day." Saikawa raised her iced tea to her lips. And then... "By the way, what were you like as a child, Kimizuka?"

That question made the other two look toward me again.

Natsunagi in particular seemed suddenly interested. "Actually, yes, I'm a bit curious about that, too. I only know what you were like after you met Siesta, Kimizuka."

"Yeah, I guess I hadn't talked about my past that much."

My childhood before I left on that journey with Siesta, and my memories from my birthdays—a few fragmented episodes that I'd shut away in the depths of my mind resurfaced for the first time in ages.

"The thing is, I don't have any interesting stories."

Those memories weren't important enough to tell anyone about, which meant that I wasn't going to say anything until someone asked.

"We're not looking for something 'interesting.'" Unexpectedly, Charlie averted her eyes and lowered the bar for me.

She wasn't the only one.

"We just want to know more about you, Kimizuka." I was drawn to Natsunagi's smile and what she said. ...Yeah, that's right. It was the same when I first met her, in that classroom after school.

"So tell us." She smiled at me gently.

Now that she'd said that, I had to do it. Hel's "word-soul"—no, Natsunagi's heartfelt words—would inexorably spur me on until I collapsed.

"The story may be a little long, is that okay?"

It just so happened that we had plenty of time before the next item on our agenda.

So, what should I start with?

I began by remembering things that had happened a few years back, one by one.

A certain girl's tale 1

"Good morning, Mistress Siesta."

After changing the water and refilling the vase with fresh water for the flowers, I set the vase down near the window, then turned to the individual who was snoozing away peacefully on the bed. The girl, *whose face was identical to my own*, was napping in the afternoon sunlight with a smile on her face.

She didn't respond to my voice. She didn't wake up. Her name—or code name, rather—was Siesta. The detective who'd saved the world.

"The calendar says it's autumn, but the days are still hot," I said. I gazed out the window, thinking of the great tree that towered somewhere, far away. Was the lingering heat of this September sun pouring down over the man and woman who'd once detested light?

Exposure to sunlight had destroyed both Seed's cells and Hel, Nagisa Natsunagi's alter who had shone brilliantly herself. The idea that those two were now in the trunk of a tree reaching up into the sky, with dazzling sunlight pouring down around them, struck me as rather ironic and sad.

They must have made peace with the sun by now, though. If they hadn't, that tree would never have grown so big. The prince and the swallow must be sleeping peacefully in the warm sunlight.

Just as Mistress Siesta was now.

"............"

I sat down in a nearby chair and looked at the white-haired girl on the bed.

After that final battle a month ago, Mistress Siesta should have reached her *happy ending*. The heart that Hel had once stolen from her had been returned, and Stephen Bluefield the Inventor had saved both her life and

Nagisa's. Then, with Kimihiko resuming his place as her assistant, she would have embarked on a new adventure.

That was the ending everyone had wanted, but one solitary thing had prevented it: the "seed" buried in her heart. Seed had given it to her, and it would continue growing as long as she was conscious. Eventually it would sprout, take over her body, and turn her into a monster.

The seed had already sunk its roots deep into her heart, and even Stephen hadn't been able to extract it. The only way to keep Mistress Siesta alive had been to render her unconscious. It was a stopgap measure, but if the seed only grew while she was awake, then we simply had to make sure she stayed asleep.

Of course, it doesn't solve the main problem. We might only be postponing an inevitable good-bye.

...Even so, I thought. Someday, we might find a way to remove that seed. The one who could do it might be an idol singer somewhere, or an agent, or the new detective, or her assistant. Someday, somebody might wake Mistress Siesta from her deep afternoon nap.

As I daydreamed about that "someday," I'd spent yet another day changing the water in the vase and gazing at Mistress Siesta's sleeping face. Our features might be identical, but my mistress's expression was far gentler than mine.

"Yes, for a little while, I'll have that sleeping face all to myself."

At present, Kimihiko Kimizuka, Nagisa Natsunagi, Yui Saikawa, and Charlotte Arisaka Anderson had left Japan for a certain country in Southeast Asia. They'd been summoned by the Federation Government, to determine whether Nagisa would be allowed to become the new Ace Detective.

The group was scheduled to return soon, provided everything went smoothly. For the past few days, as Mistress Siesta's former maid, I had been taking care of her for them.

...I'd never dreamed that I'd still be at Mistress Siesta's side at this point. "I didn't think I would live this long, either."

I had originally been an artificial intelligence created by Stephen the Inventor, who had installed me in Siesta's borrowed body. My only reason for existing had been to convey her last wish to Kimihiko and the other three, and to help them resolve their lingering issues and grow.

However, the next thing I knew, Kimihiko had declared his intent to break a taboo: He would bring Mistress Siesta back to life. Then, although it had required many sacrifices, he'd actually done it. Somewhere along the way, I had been pulled into his plan. I had unintentionally acquired a new body, and now here I was, gazing at my mistress's quiet face.

"Was this part of your plan as well, Mistress Siesta?"

Naturally, she couldn't have predicted a future in which she would be brought back to life. Even so, I had been created solely to help with her mission; it wouldn't have been odd for her to extend a helping hand out of concern for me. After all, that was the sort of detective she had been.

In addition, while the Ace Detective kept a variety of futures in mind, she treasured the past as well.

I glanced at the clock on the wall. Once I was sure that it wasn't yet time for the regular contact from Kimihiko's group, I picked up a certain journal. Mistress Siesta had given it to me earlier, through Stephen.

Information about her past was stored in my database. However, it was nice to pick up the physical book sometimes, letting my thoughts travel back in time through the blurred strokes of the ballpoint pen.

"Forgive me, Mistress Siesta. I won't show it to anyone else."

This was a memory, a record, between the two of us.

The detective's secret tale that even the assistant who'd traveled with her for three years didn't know about.

The journal began on a certain date, four years ago.

Chapter 1

◆ April 24   Siesta

"Code name: Siesta. I see you've come."

That day, in response to a summons from the Federation Government, I was visiting the Mizoev Federation's embassy in England. They'd brought me to a large room, and now I was gazing at a projected image.

Since they'd gone to the trouble of summoning me, I'd thought the individual might be here in person. However, as usual, *she* was sending this transmission from a distant foreign country. The high-ranking government official was dressed in a kimono, and she wore a mask that hid her face. "We haven't spoken face-to-face since you were appointed Ace Detective. Have you been well since then?"

Fine words from someone who wouldn't show her face. She also didn't sound particularly concerned about me. Still, that was how it always went between *my group* and *her group*. Tuners and the Federation Government had a business relationship with each other: Our greatest and only goal was to protect the world from crises.

"Yes, Ice Doll, it's been a long time," I said, responding with her code name. I hadn't taken a seat. "It's been a year since you and your people gave me the position of Ace Detective. However, understand that no matter what title I bear, it won't change what I do."

My response to her tedious greeting made the woman on the screen give a little snort. What did her face look like under that mask? Her voice made her seem fairly old, but I sensed craftiness in it, too.

"Seed's subjugation. We also pray that you will succeed in that endeavor, as the Ace Detective. Still, what is the reason for this preoccupation of yours?" Ice Doll asked.

That's right: I'd been pursuing the primordial seed longer than I'd been a Tuner. The title of Ace Detective had nothing to do with it. My mission, which I'd set for myself, was to take down Seed and his pseudohumans.

However, securing a position as a Tuner had widened my horizons considerably. I wouldn't have been able to openly own a gun otherwise. Hence, I didn't find it to be a hardship to work with the Federation Government.

"Do you have some sort of personal score to settle with the primordial seed?" I'd fallen silent, and Ice Doll pressed me for an answer.

"...I couldn't say. However, it's my mission to defeat him. It's engraved in my DNA. That's all."

Why was I so obsessed with Seed? To tell the truth, even I didn't know. However, I was missing several months' worth of memories from a certain year. I thought there must be some secret hidden within them, but those lost memories showed no sign of returning.

Even so, my instincts remembered the enemy's ominous presence. I pursued Seed, or found myself pursued by various groups for unfathomable reasons, and somewhere along the way—was it because I kept solving cases wherever I went?—I'd been given the title of Tuner and officially tasked with defeating Seed.

"And? What did you need today?" I asked, prodding Ice Doll to get to the point. I hadn't made any progress to speak of in subjugating Seed. I also hadn't been told that I was obligated to report in.

As a matter of fact, from what I'd heard, Tuners didn't have much direct contact with the Federation Government. As a rule, members of the government didn't even put in appearances at Federal Councils, the gatherings of Tuners. We Tuners were a very independent group.

"Yes. About that, Siesta." Ice Doll said. "I would like you to travel to Japan."

"...Japan? Why me?"

How was that Asian island nation related? I hadn't heard anything about Seed lurking there.

"There's a man we would like the Ace Detective to catch," Ice Doll said, and the screen changed. It now showed a photo of a man with wavy hair and a beard; he seemed to be in his late thirties. His shoes were dirty, his shirt was wrinkled, and he wore a top hat pulled down low. In the brief glimpses of his eyes, I caught sight of something like amusement. I thought back, but I couldn't remember seeing him before.

"Danny Bryant." Ice Doll's face returned, although she kept the man's photo in a corner of the screen. "He worked for the government once and is now suspected of being a spy. A year ago, he took classified information regarding the Federation Government and fled. The last place he was sighted was…"

"Japan?"

Ice Doll gave a small nod. "That's right. For the past year, we've continued searching for him using various methods, but we've run out of leads. Which is why we're requesting your help."

Indeed, depending on what information Danny had taken, this might count as a "global crisis," a job for the Tuners. But…

"When you appointed me as a Tuner last year, you told me that each great crisis was always handled by a single Tuner."

The world was constantly facing crises, and as a rule, Tuners focused on the one that had been assigned to them. Some—such as the Information Broker—supported other Tuners, but in broad terms, you could say that they also had a single job to focus on.

The role currently assigned to me as the Ace Detective was to destroy the primordial seed. And yet now, someone from the government was giving me a completely different job: apprehend a spy who had fled to Japan. Was that all right?

"As I said, this is a personal request." Ice Doll's voice hinted at a smile. "*Detective Siesta*, I would like you to accept this job for me."

…*I see*. In spite of myself, I was impressed by her approach.

For more than a year, I'd made a living by working as an ordinary detective while I pursued Seed. That was probably part of the reason they'd chosen me to be the Ace Detective. That said…

"You're going to rely on a kid? Aren't you embarrassed?"

In some countries, I was still young enough that I'd have to be in school. How stubborn would this crafty old official be with a *little girl* like me?

"You, a child? Those who've lived a life ten times more eventful than others can't be measured by the same yardstick as regular boys and girls."

"I know you're talking about mental age, but don't make me over a hundred, all right?"

"Before long, you'll understand how marvelous aging is."

I didn't really trust the person who'd said that, so I couldn't just easily agree.

If the Information Broker had made that remark, for example, would I have believed it? If I recalled correctly, he'd lived twice as long as the average human. As a matter of fact, since I was still young, the world was probably bursting with things I hadn't seen yet.

"...All right. I'll accept the request."

I wasn't entirely convinced, but if she was asking for my help as a detective, I didn't really have a choice. Besides, finding people is what detectives do best. I committed Danny's face to memory. She didn't even have to send me the data; I could remember that much.

"I thought you would."

There she went again. I had a hunch I'd been cleverly tricked, but either way, I'd wanted to visit Japan. This might be a perfect opportunity.

"...Why did I want to go to Japan?"

Out of nowhere, that question crossed my mind. I had vaguely felt that I'd always wanted to, but now that I was thinking about it, I had no idea why. Why did something about that country strike me as nostalgic?

"We'll book a flight for the day after tomorrow. Can you be ready by then?"

Ice Doll didn't seem to have heard me talking to myself. On the other side of the screen, she'd begun typing on a keyboard.

"No, make it the first flight tomorrow," I said, and the woman's hands paused. "I only have one trunk. I'm always ready to go anywhere, at any time."

"...How reassuring."

I had thought about going to that clock tower in London this evening, though. I wouldn't be seeing the younger Tuner who lived there for a while. In this day and age, there were countless ways to get in touch long-distance, but I thought I'd at least have a farewell party before I left. ...Although I suspect she'd probably cry a whole lot.

Actually, would she have predicted this already? Assuming my departure counted as a global crisis to her, that is.

"By the way, may I ask one thing?" On the screen, the official was preparing to leave the room when I spoke. "What sort of classified information did this Danny Bryant fellow steal?"

There was silence for a few seconds.

If a high-ranking government official was willing to make a *personal request* to find him, what sort of important Federation Government secrets had this spy gotten his hands on? Since I'd taken the job, I wanted her to tell me at least that much. However...Ice Doll said nothing.

"...So you can't tell me at this point?"

Her silence was my answer.

"In that case, if I manage to bring him here, tell me then," I said, adding that would be my compensation for taking on her request.

Considering the size of the job, they should let me get away with being a little underhanded.

"You really aren't a child." Ice Doll smiled coldly.

"No, I'm still young enough to enjoy playing make-believe, ma'am." Being carefully polite, I turned on my heel and started to leave. "By the way..." I began, assuming the official was still glaring at me on the screen behind me. "How is life in the Mizoev Federation?"

Silence fell again. There was no answer.

In that case, I didn't have time to waste on this. Keeping my back to the screen, I began to walk away.

"Well, it's marvelous, simply wonderful," she said casually. "I'd like to invite you here as well someday."

I was sure she didn't mean a word of it.

After that, I visited the clock tower where my dear protégé lived. After I told her I'd be leaving the country for a while (She cried, as I'd thought she would. It was adorable), I returned to my apartment and packed.

It was a furnished apartment with its own appliances, so it didn't take me long to get ready to leave. I simply packed my personal belongings into my trunk, and that was that. Now all I'd have to do tomorrow morning was leave for the airport.

"I guess I won't be seeing this town again for a while."

I opened the window and looked out at the street, which was illuminated by a bright full moon. I felt a little guilty about leaving my precious protégé by herself, but... Either way, since I'd be fighting SPES in earnest from now on, this secondment might be a perfect opportunity.

"It's cold."

In England, the night wind was still chilly at this time of year. I closed the window and drew the curtains.

It was about time I went to bed. If I was late for my flight after boldly declaring I was ready to go, I'd tarnish the name of the Ace Detective. With that thought in mind, I walked toward my bed— And just then, I felt a breeze on my back. Even though I'd closed the window.

"Lock up carefully. The wolves come out at night."

Had I forgotten to lock it? No, things like that were probably useless in *his* case. Sighing, I made my way to my bed and crawled under the covers.

"Ignoring me? How cruel. Or are you implying that you want the wolf to attack you?"

The man was as talkative as ever.

Reluctantly, I sat up in bed. "You're not a werewolf, Scarlet. You're a vampire."

A man in a white suit was leaning against the wall in a dark corner of the room. Blood stained the corners of his lips.

"Hm? Oh, excuse me. I haven't killed anyone, mind you." Registering my gaze, Scarlet wiped the blood away with his handkerchief and defended himself. "Someone only shared a little blood with me. If that was forbidden, too, I wouldn't be able to survive in this world." Pointing out that he didn't have much choice, Scarlet tried to justify his actions. I knew he didn't choose to live this way because he wanted to, but I wasn't in any position to decide whether it was right or wrong to begin with.

"And? What do you need? It's late," I said, giving a little yawn. Granted, he only ever appeared at night anyway.

"Does a husband need a reason to visit his wife?"

There he went again. I'd first met Scarlet a year ago, at my first-ever Federal Council. He'd been a Tuner much, much longer than I had. Ever since he first laid eyes on me, he'd taken every chance he could find to talk to me, and at this point he was shamelessly stalking me. I'd heard that he was based in London now. It couldn't be because I was there, could it?

"How old are you? People are going to start calling you a pedophile."

I wasn't old enough to get married yet anyway. ...Although that might not be true in some countries.

"To vampires, all humans are babes in arms." Scarlet gave a smug smile. That's one of his specialties: smiling pretentiously despite being completely uncool. "Any bride of mine must be strong. That's an absolute requirement. And you meet it."

I wasn't so sure. In terms of female Tuners, Fuubi was definitely better than me.

"What do you say? If you'll be my woman, I'll give you half the world."

"You've played too many RPGs," I said by way of refusal.

Scarlet gave another little laugh and went over to the window. Then... "I hear the higher-ups said something to you."

His tone had changed slightly. He meant my exchange with Ice Doll. Apparently, that was the reason behind his visit.

"Were you lurking in a shadow to eavesdrop?"

"Ha! If only." Scarlet gave a thin smile. "If I could travel between shadows like the vampires found in fiction, I'd have it much easier." He can make it look like he's melting into the shadows, but he can't make it happen for real.

The wings he usually kept inside his body created those illusions. They can generate several hundred million patterns of light and darkness, bending light at will and tricking the human eye into believing that Scarlet has emerged from the shadows, or vanished into them. The unreality of vampires is a product of science. Yes, his kind was originally created by—

"We are not their slaves."

Standing under the window and its moonlit view, Scarlet gazed at me. By "their," he probably meant the Federation Government officials. Had he been listening from the other side of the door? Or had he intercepted the transmission? He didn't seem happy about the conversation I'd had with Ice Doll. "The Federation Government and the Tuners are supposed to be equal, independent organizations. If they are giving you orders, there must be something behind it."

No, it wasn't dissatisfaction. It was more like...

"If they're unjustly making you obey, I'll—"

"It's all right." I rejected the proposal before Scarlet finished. "I accepted this job of my own free will, as a detective."

Not as the Ace Detective.

"Detectives are earnest in every age, I see." Scarlet gave a pointed shrug. Seeing him do things like this made me think he was no different from humans. ...Although I had no idea whether a vampire would be happy to hear that.

"Don't overwork or overestimate yourself. There are countless heroes in this world, far more than just the Tuners. If one of us cuts corners, it won't be much of an issue."

It sounded as if Scarlet hadn't really understood what I meant. I wasn't acting as a Tuner at all; my actions were driven by my own personal sense of mission. ...Or maybe he was trying to tell me that I didn't need to be bound by that type of justice, either. In any case...

"Thank you for worrying about me."

I seemed to have caught Scarlet by surprise. His golden eyes widened slightly. "Letting you go really would be a waste." His surprise softened into an expression of regret.

It's not as if you ever caught me in the first place.

Then, with his usual smug smile, Scarlet sprouted black wings.

"You're going already?" I asked, guessing the vampire had said all he'd come to say.

"I'm off to kill my people again."

That was the mission Scarlet had been assigned.

"It's for the sake of a noble cause."

Why had Scarlet, who didn't like the humans of the Federation Government and the same man who'd told me there was no need to be bound by justice, accepted the duty of killing his fellow vampires on the pretext of "a noble cause"?

How many people actually knew the answer to that?

"Who does this 'noble cause' of yours really benefit?"

At this point, the vampire's large back told me nothing.

He'd told me about *his plan* once, though, and I did know a few things.

One: No living human could become the "bride" he spoke of.

Two: When he said, "I'll give you half the world," he'd been completely serious.

Three: The fact that he would become an enemy of the world was already written in the sacred text.

The rest was my own deduction.

If I defeated Seed someday, the next mission the Ace Detective was assigned would probably be—

"The world's orbit is out of alignment—but a day will come when it is corrected."

Setting his hand on the window, Scarlet looked back.

"On that day, I would like my precious bride to watch and see which of us disappears, at least."

◆ April 26   Siesta

In the arrivals lobby of the airport after my flight from England, the first thing I had to do—with my carry-on bag in one hand—was answer the phone nonstop. "All right. ...Yes. Yes, okay, go ahead and rent the shop."

I'd just finished a twelve-hour flight, and now I had to return all the calls that had come in while I was on the plane. That had been the last of them, though. I'd probably be in Japan for a while, so I'd just arranged for a place to stay.

"—It's Japan."

Once I'd ended the call, I started to hear the noises of the crowd around me.

Naturally, everyone was speaking Japanese, and I felt a twinge of nostalgia—although I couldn't say why. It was true that I'd visited Japan a few times before, but had any of those memories been vivid enough to make me homesick?

I was thinking about it rather absently, when—

"Bwuff!"

Bwuff?

Looking down, I saw the face of a little girl near my stomach. She'd been running around, and she'd crashed into me before she could stop.

"Are you all right? It's okay. You're fine, it doesn't hurt," I said. I crouched down to be at the same eye level as her.

She looked about five years old, and her flushed cheeks were as soft as mochi. *Oh, she is going to cry,* I thought immediately.

"...Daddy's gone."

Ah, so she was lost. That's why she'd been running around in a panic.

Her voice was hoarse, and somehow, just taking her to the information center didn't feel right.

"Why don't you come over here with me?"

The airport lobby was crowded. Holding the little girl's hand, I found an empty bench, had her sit down, then handed her a drink I'd bought from a vending machine. Her eyes lit up, and she started to gulp it down, holding the can with both hands. She must have been really thirsty; she was swallowing noisily.

Just as I was about to ask if it tasted good, it hit me: For the past few minutes, I'd been speaking Japanese quite naturally.

...That's right. I'd spoken Japanese with a friend like this, long ago. Maybe that explained the nostalgia.

"...A friend?"

A friend who spoke Japanese.

Who on earth had it been?

When had I had friends?

"Lady? Are you okay? It's okay." The little girl was watching me in confusion.

Good grief. Now I'd made a lost child worry about me. Pathetic.

"Where did you lose your dad?" I asked as gently as I could, trying my best not to sound like I was interrogating her.

"Near the souvenir shop," she answered. "Daddy's always wandering off." She insisted that her father was the one who'd strayed away. "When I asked the people in the store, they said he'd left his wallet at the cash register."

That was her story, and she was sticking to it.

However, in the wallet the girl had shown me, I found a note with an address and telephone number. What a practical parent. In that case, calling the phone number would probably solve this. I took out my smartphone, but...

"He isn't picking up."

Was he looking for his daughter so frantically that he hadn't noticed the call?

I really wished the human race would hurry up and evolve the power of telepathy.

"Do you think he's okay?" The girl was starting to look uneasy again. She was holding a pack of candy and had chocolate smeared around her mouth. Had she lost sight of her father while she was sampling it, or in the middle of buying souvenirs?

"Shall we go look for the souvenir shop?"

I'd just taken the girl's hand and gotten to my feet when—

"Oh! Mommy!"

Slipping free from my fingers, the girl ran toward a woman. So her mom had been here, too.

It seems there wouldn't be any need for a detective this time. Well, that was fine. With a small sigh of relief, I started to walk away.

"I found Daddy," the girl's mother said.

My legs froze. When I looked back, a man who didn't seem much older than forty had joined the two of them. "Sorry for the trouble," he said, smiling wryly.

Early-onset dementia.

The little girl's father really had been the one who was lost. The mother had found him somewhere and brought him back.

The note with the address and phone number had been in the wallet as a safeguard for an individual with dementia, just in case they wandered off. Since I'd heard the story from a child, I'd ignored her claims and thought of a situation that worked using my own common sense instead.

"That was a terrible mistake to make as a detective, wasn't it?"

Yeah, I'd flunked this one.

I still had a long way to go. I was nowhere near perfect. My hands couldn't quite pull a client back to safety from the edge of a cliff. My eyes weren't trained enough to spot people buried under rubble.

At this point, I needed to doubt my own common sense.

Or rather, maybe because it was common sense, the idea of doubting it hadn't even occurred to me.

Then what should I do? Think. Think. Think, come up with a hypothesis, test it, fail again probably, and finally find the answer. I'd keep improving myself, day after day, and become a detective who could protect her clients' interests. One who could make wishes come true.

"Right now, I have a job to do."

After I'd watched the family leave, I took out my phone again. Now that I'd landed in Japan, I'd been tasked with finding a man named Danny Bryant who'd disappeared a year ago.

At present, I had no clues whatsoever. I needed a lead. On that thought, I called a certain acquaintance.

"Hello. Would you like to have tea with me?'

An hour later.

Once I'd taken a taxi to my next destination, I promptly met up with the person I'd just called, and the two of us had tea together like old friends. …Or that was how it should have gone.

"I'm impressed you had the nerve to walk through that door."

We were in a reception room at the police station. The other guest at my tea party was sitting across from me, drumming her fingers on the table in an irritated manner.

"Don't be so cold. The two of us go way back."

"Yeah, we've tried to kill each other and everything." The woman—a redheaded police officer—abruptly pulled a gun and pointed it at me.

Now and even back then, I've always been the one who seemed likely to get killed. "If you're going to draw a weapon, shouldn't you consider where you are first?"

"Conveniently, this room has no security cameras."

"They'll figure it out from the noise."

"I've got a silencer. It won't be a problem."

"Isn't the fact that you've modified a department-issued gun enough of a problem already?"

She was still scowling, but she settled back into her seat. This officer, who wasn't behaving like a police officer at all, was Fuubi Kase.

Publicly, she was a Japanese policewoman, but she had a second, private identity as the globe-trotting Assassin. Like me, Fuubi Kase was a Tuner.

As the Assassin, most of her jobs consisted of killing targets on orders from the Federation Government. As one of those targets, I'd spent my days fleeing from her.

Personally, I considered our past to be water under the bridge. I wanted to cooperate and get along as work colleagues, but Fuubi seemed to still have beef with me. "First you slipped through my fingers, and now you're a fellow Tuner. What are the higher-ups thinking?"

The focus of her annoyance shifted; the government officials who'd ordered my assassination had turned around and made me one of their pawns, and she didn't like that, either. With an aggressive flick of her

lighter, she lit a cigar. "And you—how are you okay with this? You're getting worked like a dog by the same people who ordered a hit on you."

Good point. If that were the whole picture, I seemed like an incredibly accommodating person. But...

"The fact that they were after my life helped me come up with a big theory about a possibility that had always worried me."

Fuubi gazed steadily at me, as if she was trying to figure out what I was after.

"When you and your people started targeting me, I was hunting Seed for personal reasons. That should have been considered the right thing to do, yet there you were, the symbol of justice, trying to kill me. I couldn't understand it. ...Not at first." I took a sip of my tea. "After thinking it through, I deduced it must be because my survival would benefit Seed. I could become a vessel that would help him survive. You were trying to kill me before that happened."

I was missing several months' worth of memories. They were probably memories of the days I'd spent with Seed, at that facility his people had built. However, it wasn't until Fuubi started trying to kill me that I realized I might have been cultivated as Seed's vessel.

"As a result, I'm actually grateful to you. Because you attempted to eliminate me, I managed to puzzle out my own identity."

The Federation Government had tried to wither Seed indirectly by killing me. However, when I kept defying their expectations and escaping from the Assassin, they'd decided to make me a Tuner and send me to subjugate Seed instead. If you looked at it that way, there was nothing inconsistent about it.

"Well, aren't you mature." Fuubi dully exhaled a puff of smoke.

In that case, everything from this point on would be childish nonsense.

"There's just one thing that bothers me," I said. Fuubi turned to look at me. "Our superiors ordered you to assassinate me because I was Seed's vessel. How do you suppose they knew that?"

They had the Oracles' sacred text, which foretold all threats to the world. I'd heard it was hard for even the government's people to get a look at it, though.

The other day, Ice Doll didn't seem to be aware of the history Seed and I shared. Had that only been an act? Or did someone else know the truth, and they simply hadn't told her?

"Don't tell me you're asking me to look into all of that for you. Is that why you came here?" Fuubi seemed extremely annoyed at the prospect.

"No, I know this isn't the time to obsess over something like that." My main objective was defeating Seed, nothing more.

And my current job was...

"Danny Bryant."

When she heard that name, Fuubi froze for a second. Then she stubbed out her cigar in the ashtray.

"You heard of him?" I asked, although I hardly needed to.

He was a former Federation Government spy who'd abruptly disappeared in Japan a year ago. Fuubi was a Tuner who worked in Japan as a police officer. There was no way she didn't know about him.

"So they gifted you with that pain in the butt, too, huh?" Fuubi sighed heavily.

"...Meaning they've sent the job to you before?"

"Yeah, well. I told them I was busy and bowed out partway through."

"I see. So then it was my turn." So this woman was part of the reason I'd been sent all the way to Japan. "What do you know about Danny?" If this had been her job previously, she had to have at least some information.

"He came to Japan about three years ago. Then, last year, he vanished."

"What did he do in the meantime? I don't mean as a spy; what was his cover story?"

"From what I hear, he was a private detective of sorts. Like you." Fuubi smiled. She told me he'd worked as a detective and had been covertly doing something for the government on the side.

Did he come to Japan because of his second job? That part was probably classified; even Ice Doll wouldn't tell me about it.

"It seemed he didn't have a permanent office. It's not clear how he got work."

"Where did he live, then? He must have slept somewhere." ...Although I frequently didn't have a fixed address myself.

"He wandered here, there, and everywhere. We've traced him to places all around Japan. Every single one of 'em is deserted now, but he stayed in this city, too."

Taking out a laptop, Fuubi showed me a list of places where Danny Bryant had lived temporarily. They ranged from Okinawa all the way up to

Hokkaido. At least for the two years he'd spent in Japan, he never had a fixed address.

As a matter of fact, both of Danny's jobs had probably demanded that sort of flexibility. In spite of his long, shaggy hair, worn-out shirt, and loosened tie—for some reason, he still had that gleam of amusement in his eyes. Wondering if he'd been a freewheeling character from the beginning, I caught myself putting together a profile for this target I'd never even met.

"—No, that's just common sense." I promptly shook my head. I couldn't let myself be limited by that again.

A free spirit who didn't care about his appearance, whose occupation was unknown and had no permanent address. That wasn't necessarily his true nature. There was a decent possibility that *he was just making it look that way*. And...although he seemed to be a free spirit, he might not have been a lone wolf.

"Did Danny Bryant have family?"

Maybe he was a spy, and maybe he had no fixed address. Even so, deciding that he had no family based on those things would have been premature.

"As far as I know, this guy had no relatives during the time he lived in Japan. But..." Fuubi's nose wrinkled as she told me about *a certain boy* Danny had been looking after. "From what I hear, Danny Bryant used to live here in town with this one problem kid. You wouldn't even believe the amount of trouble he causes for me... Well, perfect timing: You should know it, too. That damn brat's name is—"

◇ April 27   Kimihiko Kimizuka

That day, as usual, I'd gotten dragged into a car chase.

"Whoa...!"

It might have been "the usual" for me, but no matter how used to something your brain is, it doesn't necessarily mean your body can keep up.

It was a scene straight out of an action movie: The sports car's windshield was already smashed, and I was clinging to the grab handle as the car whipped around, jostling me back and forth in the passenger seat.

"Ha-ha! Other cars are stopping to watch. Am I in the zone or what?"

Even in this situation, there was one guy who refused to remember where we were. He was next to me, behind the steering wheel, laughing as we pulled ahead of our pursuers.

"They're stunned because we're driving the wrong way!"

He was ignoring traffic lights and violating the speed limit. We hadn't hit any actual people, but our car was flying down a major street; the only phrase for what we were doing was "reckless endangerment."

"The wrong way? In the country I'm from, cars drive on the right."

"This is Japan! Would you get that through your head alr—"

Just then, our car whipped around a hundred and eighty degrees.

"—! I almost bit my tongue!"

"Ha-ha! You did, huh?! You should grab yourself a spare for next time."

"And you should quit running your mouth off, Danny!" I shot a resentful look at the man in the driver's seat.

The man's name was Danny Bryant.

He was my guarantor, the one who'd showed up abruptly one day a few years back and claimed to be my relative.

He'd pulled me out of the children's home and brought me to his apartment, but he took off on his own all the time. He was an enigmatic wanderer who'd come back once or twice a month with all these weird souvenirs. The only things I knew about him were that he was originally from America, and that he was around forty.

According to Danny, he was a "jack of all trades." He'd take on any job, from finding a neighbor's lost cat to a cold murder case the police had given up on. I didn't know how much of this was true, but he said his policy was to dash over to anywhere that wanted him and do whatever they needed. As a result, he had places all over Japan—or actually, all over the world—and he had me live at one of them.

I had no idea why Danny had approached me, but I'd used him to get by, earning a living by helping out with the jobs he brought in from time to time.

I did have one big gripe about him, though. In summer, he'd take me to a deserted island and give a flowery spiel about the secrets of survival, and in winter, we'd climb a snow-covered mountain and he'd drum into me the powerlessness of humans. Every time he did this stuff, he'd talk about his personal philosophy, but frankly, it never made much of an impression on me. Danny Bryant was a sketchy guy with a penchant for carelessness.

"Damn, they sure are stubborn." Glancing at our pursuers in the rear-view mirror, Danny pulled out a lighter and lit a cigarette. "They were sitting on a fortune. All we did was help ourselves to a little of it, and the whole office is chasing after us." Danny sighed. "Are they bored, or do they just really like money?"

"That's not a line thieves should be saying."

"Ha-ha! I was hired to redistribute wealth, that's all."

All these shiny black cars were chasing us because Danny had stolen money from them. ...Not that he'd done it for personal gain. These guys were loan sharks, and some of their victims had hired Danny to steal back the money they'd been scammed out of. If you were to put a positive spin on it, you could have called him a modern-day Robin Hood, I guess. But...

"Wasn't there a slightly smoother way to take the money back? Like quietly cracking their safe, maybe?"

Our actual approach had been to have me visit the loan sharks' office, pretending to be a client. As the sharks were taking the money out of the safe, Danny had thrown up a smoke screen, charged in, and robbed them.

"The safe was opened. That's good enough, isn't it? What matters is what actually happened and the outcome," Danny said, laughing it off. "Most of the time, the key to resolving problems isn't something you've personally got."

"You leave all the important stuff to somebody else, huh."

"Ha-ha. I just believe in people, that's all."

...There he goes again, wrapping things up in random ways.

And the "outcome" had been this hour-long car chase. Danny was always getting on somebody's bad side and chased like this, while I usually got dragged into the mess.

"If somebody's chasing you, it means you're somebody worth chasing." Danny grinned proudly for no apparent reason, stroking his beard with his fingers.

"Nope. Your sayings are shallower than a mud puddle."

"Ha-ha! Well, they're just words. If there was a saying with the fathom-less depths of a swamp, letting it tie you down would be a whole lot dumber. Don't trust what people say," he said bluntly.

As always, the guy had a pat response for everything.

"You really never smile, kid," Danny griped, still looking ahead with his hands on the wheel. "Have you ever grinned for real, even once?"

"Leave me alone. This is just how I look."

"Ha! You're sure you're not just imagining that?" Cutting the wheel, he veered off the broad avenue onto a side street. "Nobody knows what their genuine self is like. The real you might actually be a friendly, smiley kid."

Who knows? The dark humor in my favorite gangster movie leaves me in stitches every time I see it, but that's about it.

"As long as you're yanking me around and dragging me into trouble, you're only ever going to see smiles of pain."

"Ha-ha. For an apprentice, you sure aren't cute!"

"Who's your apprentice, and when did that happen?"

"Hm? Oh, right. Are you my son, then?"

"That's even less likely. Are you telling me my name's actually Kimihiko Bryant Kimizuka?"

I was born with black hair and Japanese features, and I looked nothing like this sketchy guy. Why had he even said he was a relative?

"True, we're not related by blood, but I'm your father figure. ...Uh, actually, maybe 'teacher' sounds cooler." Danny smiled cheerfully.

Okay, the happy-go-lucky thing is great, but are we going to be able to lose those guys?

"Don't worry. You've got me on your team now." He grinned, trying to reassure me.

Should I tell him *That's why I'm worried: because you're here?*

"Listen up, kid." Without waiting for my retort, Danny spoke calmly, one hand on the wheel. "You're bound to run into all sorts of enemies in life: gangsters and spies, sickening criminals, and great evils you can't even begin to imagine."

"Enemies? What kind of life am I going to have?"

"Hey, you're young, and it's already like this. Action movies are only the beginning."

Yeah, that doesn't bode well. I gave my usual forced smile.

Getting pulled into an incident like this one right before my birthday seemed pretty unnecessary.

"Still, don't worry," Danny repeated. "You'll get dragged into all manner of trouble, run into all kinds of enemies, and come up against all sorts of danger, but whenever it happens, someone's guaranteed to show up and go through it with you. That's what's been decided."

After that, we managed to get ourselves out of that problem. Now our car was parked beside a certain house.

"So this is the client's place...?" I looked at the house through the passenger-side window. It seemed old.

Part of the money Danny had retrieved from the loan sharks had been paid in by the family that lived here. They'd lost three million yen to illegal interest. The cash we'd stolen from the moneylenders' office was in an attaché case in the back seat.

Of course, no matter how you tried to whitewash it, this money game was a crime. If we got caught, we were finished. At the very least, we couldn't let anybody find out about the connection between Danny and the client. Danny always said he was the only one whose job description included getting caught by the yakuza and the cops. ...Although, according to him, neither had ever caught him yet.

"I wish you'd quit using me as a body double," I grumbled quietly.

Enemies who'd been after Danny had gone after me when I was alone several times before. Worried that this might end up being one of those occasions, I looked at the driver's seat.

—However.

"Shh." Danny looked more serious than I'd ever seen him.

When I hastily strained my ears, I heard something in the distance. It was coming from that house. A woman's shrill, angry voice, and the sound of dishes shattering. Then a child crying.

"Domestic trouble, huh?"

I understood right away. This sort of thing happened when families were poverty stricken. The facility where I'd lived had taken in kids from homes like that pretty frequently.

"It's daytime, but they've shut those thick curtains. There must be something in there that they don't want people seeing." Next to me, Danny analyzed the family's situation. "They haven't been taking care of their yard, either. That's proof they don't have that kind of time or emotional energy. When the parents are in that state, guess who they take it out on."

He didn't have to say more than that.

I started to ask him what we were going to do, but then I broke off. Next to me, his profile was suffused with anger. "Kids can't choose their parents." Danny was glaring at something, or someone, that wasn't there. "Parents are all kids have. And yet..." He tightened his grip on the steering wheel.

Those words sounded simple, but when I really thought about them, they were true. Parents were active members of society, so they had a world outside their home and connections to other people. Children only had their parents. All they could do as they grew up was follow behind and watch. All kids... All *we* could count on were our parents.

"And yet I—" Danny was gazing into the distance.

Every so often, every once in a while, he would do that.

I'd never asked him why.

"What should we do? Should we call the police?"

Right now, there was nothing for it but to do what we had to do.

I took out my phone. Would this go faster if I called my usual police station?

"No, a visit from the cops would just be a temporary fix. What actually solves problems is always *this*."

Danny seemed to have calmed down a little, or maybe he'd given up. Rubbing his fingers together in the gesture for "money," he gave a world-weary smile. And then... "What do you think? Do I look like a lawyer?" Stroking his whiskers, Danny checked his reflection in the rearview mirror. Apparently, he was planning to pass himself off as one when he gave them the money.

"If you're trying to look like the manager of a law office that's always in the red, I think you can probably skate by." If he wanted to look like a decent lawyer, he'd need to shine his shoes and buy a new suit, to start with.

"Is it really okay to give them this money, though? What if the loan sharks track us here?"

These people were already having trouble at home. What would happen to them then? I had a bad feeling, and I didn't think it was just paranoia.

"No need to worry about that. I'll have a guard here for a while." Danny pointed at a young man in a dark suit who was just walking past the house. "Passerby A, who walks in front of this house every hour. That's *their* job, this time around."

Giving me an explanation that didn't make much sense, Danny grabbed the attaché case from the back seat. "Besides, clearing up the trouble that's right under our noses comes first." He reached for the door handle. "Kids have a future, and their lives take priority every time." Turning halfway back, he gave me a smile. It looked as if he wanted to say something.

"What about me, then?"

I'm a kid, and the loan sharks might hunt me down because of this, you know?

"Ha-ha! Call it proof that I trust you. You won't die that easy."

With that optimistic declaration, Danny headed to work.

Yeah. Thanks to that, he always lets me do whatever I want.

◆ April 28   Siesta

"Nice. This came out even better than I expected."

Having put on a certain item that had been delivered that morning, I examined myself in the bathroom mirror and sighed with amazement.

My face had been my constant companion for over a decade. Who would have thought it could look so different without plastic surgery?

Right now, I was the very image of a Japanese woman in her late twenties. Once I changed out of my usual dress, it was likely that even people who knew me wouldn't recognize me.

"That's *the Inventor* for you. He does good work."

I stroked my face—well, the *mask* that clung to my skin—with my fingertips. The mask fit the contours of my face so well it didn't even feel like I was wearing anything. It was as if I'd applied the sort of special effects makeup they use in movies.

Currently, I was a detective on a mission to find a spy who'd fled to this country. That meant it was necessary to act covertly, so I'd had an acquaintance prepare a mask for me.

The Inventor had made several handy items for me before. At this rate, I might be able to get a full set of seven tools, like a real detective.

"What else would be good? A gun, maybe?"

An ordinary firearm would be pointless. I'd also prefer something that looked cooler than what I was using now. If I left its performance to the Inventor, I was sure I wouldn't end up with something weird.

"Could I use boots with hidden shoe lifts to change my height?"

This mask couldn't change my figure, but I could probably manage something with accessories. With a voice changer, I could make my voice do anything I wanted. Now I could finally get down to business. Stepping away from the sink in high spirits, I went back into the *shop*.

"I may have gone overboard in assembling my collection."

The small, old shop was packed with antiques and pieces of fine art I'd picked up over the past few days. I'd learned that the spy I was after, Danny Bryant, tended to collect those kinds of things. Maybe it was a hobby.

Naturally, this was just to help my mood. I wasn't seriously hoping that he might stop by one day if I pretended to run an antique store. However, I did think that putting myself in the target's shoes might let me see things I hadn't been able to see before. So I'd rented a shop in the city where Danny had once lived, and I planned to treat it as my base of operations while I was living in Japan.

"Now then, what should I do next?"

All I'd done over the past few days was make basic preparations. My investigation was about to begin in earnest. Should I start with Kimihiko Kimizuka, the boy I'd heard about?

Danny Bryant had been looking after "Boy K.," and coincidentally, the kid still lived in town. I called Fuubi again, hoping for more information on him.

"Hello? About that boy you mentioned earlier, the one who always gets dragged into things…"

"I'm busy. Hanging up," a cranky voice said three seconds into the call. Then she hung up.

And then she called me right back.

"Never talk about that guy where I can hear you."

"If you're going that far, now I'm really curious." I wanted to see him today, right away.

"Ha! If you want to meet that damn brat, you don't even have to try. Just walk around town and you'll run into him."

Fuubi was probably referring to what she'd said earlier: Boy K. had *a knack for getting dragged into trouble.* If there was an incident, he was sure to turn up.

That said, could I count on an incident happening so conveniently?

Fuubi seemed to know what I was thinking. "Stuff happens so often there's no time to sleep." She sighed, then listed several cases she was currently working on. "So, like I said, I'm busy. Go see the rest for yourself." She hung up wearily.

What did you have to do to get a police officer to hate you this much? I smiled with some chagrin. I'd never met Boy K., but he was sounding more and more intriguing.

That said, if I couldn't rely on a real policewoman any longer—

"I'll just have to count on a fake one."

An hour later...

"Mm-hmm. That went well."

I'd gotten Boy K.'s current address from city hall in record time, and I was in a good mood as I walked through town.

As I passed by an elderly woman, she said, "Thank you for your service."

It was the clothes. Right now, no matter who saw me, I looked like a *police officer*. I'd used that mask to change my face, while the odds and ends I was always collecting for undercover investigations had come in handy for my uniform.

My strategy had been simple: I'd visited city hall disguised as a police officer and told them I needed Boy K.'s personal information for an investigation. A certain notebook had also come in handy. It had been issued by the Federation Government, and it gave me all sorts of credentials to get into places the average person wasn't allowed to go, and public institutions provided me with information more easily. If I wanted to conduct detective work using the shortest possible route, this was an essential item.

"What's that you say? Why cosplay as a police officer, then? Oh, this is fan service," I said, in response to a question no one had actually asked, and then I reached the apartment building.

I climbed the rusty stairs and rang the doorbell of Boy K.'s apartment... but there was no answer.

"And of course it's locked."

I twisted the knob, just to check, but the door didn't open. The electrical meter was turning, but only very slowly; apparently, he wasn't just pretending to not be home. That said, there wasn't a buildup of flyers in the mailbox, which meant the apartment's resident came home regularly.

"I see. School, huh?"

It was a weekday. I didn't go to school, so I'd forgotten about it. In that case, would it be faster to visit the schools in this district? ...But I'd come all the way here; it felt like a waste. All of a detective's actions should have meaning.

When you're reading a mystery novel and an important-looking character or item shows up but is never explained, it's a letdown. In the same way, I wanted to be responsible and make sure everything I did meant something. Because, yes—I am a detective.

"And so, excuse the intrusion."

Using *a certain special key*, I boldly let myself into Boy K.'s apartment.

It was a master key the Inventor had given me, just after I'd been appointed Ace Detective. With the exception of electronic locks, there's no door it can't open. From what I'd been told, it was the custom for this key to be handed down from Ace Detective to Ace Detective.

"Everything from this point on is typical detective work."

The Ace Detective and the Assassin stood on the front line with support from other Tuners. That was how our roles were divided. ...Although what I was about to do was nothing that grand.

And so, while the tenant was away, I went in to look for any traces Danny Bryant might have left behind.

In the kitchen, I found an unwashed cup, plus the last two slices of a loaf of bread sitting on top of the microwave. The living room was littered with clothes. The place felt lived-in; I could tell someone was here most of the time, and they'd just stepped out temporarily.

One other thing about the apartment caught my attention: The rather small living room held a whole lot of antiques and souvenirs from around the country. The carved wooden bear on the shelf, for example. That probably wasn't Boy K.'s taste. Danny Bryant couldn't still be living here, could he? If he was, I couldn't imagine Fuubi not noticing it, but...

At the very least, these things were probably supporting evidence that he'd been here once. On that thought, I inspected the room carefully. Assuming Boy K. wasn't a juvenile delinquent, one empty beer can or cigarette butt might prove that Danny Bryant was still here... But nothing turned up even after going through the trash bins.

Parenthetically, I did find magazines with lots of pictures of swimsuit-clad women in the closet, but I had a hunch that those probably were Boy K.'s, so I lined them up on the bookshelf for him.

"I guess that's all I'm going to find here."

There was no material evidence.

In that case, I should get some witness testimonies next. I left the apartment and set off to find Boy K.

"If this is his address, then first..."

I didn't know whether Boy K. went to a public school or a private one, so I decided to try them all, starting with the closest one. This uniform and my notebook would let me gather information more efficiently.

The incident happened while I was on my way to the closest middle school, with those thoughts still running through my head.

"Whoa!"

A figure dashed out of a mixed-use building and almost ran straight into me.

It was a young man in a tacky, expensive suit. His head was shaved, and his wide-open collar exposed tattooed skin. Usually, when a guy like that sees a police officer, he would quietly look away. —But.

"Are you a cop?! Somebody's dead in there!"

Unexpectedly, the man clung to me. Wide-eyed, he pointed at a room in the mixed-use building, his hand shaking. Its curtains were open. Apparently, the incident took place on the third floor.

Without waiting for the man to show me the way, I dashed into the building. I ran upstairs, taking the steps two at a time, and opened the door to a place that looked like a consumer loan office.

"——!"

In the back of the room, a big man who had to be one hundred and ninety centimeters tall was lying on the ground, bleeding from his chest.

Beside him stood a boy with a slight build. He was holding a knife, and his expression seemed rather lonely and melancholy. ...Or maybe resigned. As if he'd given up entirely.

"Kid. What's your name?"

Even I don't know why that was the first question I asked him.

He looked as if he'd been left behind, all alone in the world. His profile was so sad, and yet somehow, I couldn't take my eyes off him. I may have just wanted to know his name more than anything else.

"I'm—"

In the next moment, I remembered what that redheaded policewoman had said.

If you want to meet him, just walk around town.

"Kimihiko Kimizuka."

That was how I met Boy K.

A certain boy's tale 2

"So you had a surrogate dad, Kimizuka…"

We were still in that restaurant, with the summer wind blowing through. When my story reached a stopping point, Natsunagi exhaled. I guess she wasn't expecting that.

I'd told them about a certain day a few years back, when Danny and I had been in a car chase, up until we gave the client the money we'd retrieved from the loan sharks. And in order to tell that story, I'd also had to tell them about how I'd met Danny and what he was like.

I'd never mentioned him to Natsunagi before, though. Saikawa and Charlie hadn't heard about him either, and the story seemed to catch them off guard.

"Kimizuka, you were reckless even before you met Ma'am." Charlie narrowed her eyes at me.

Well, I'm pretty sure Charlie and I weren't much different there.

"Blame it on my predisposition; it didn't start with Siesta. I've been involved in this stuff since I was born." I didn't want to write that off with a simple, *So I'm used to it*, though.

"They say the gods don't give people trials they can't overcome, right? That's what this is," Charlie said. She primly sipped her drink. "Better tell them thank you."

"If that's true, then the gods of this world are total sadists, don't you think?"

"That doesn't get me excited. I'm not Nagisa."

"Wh-who did you say was such a masochist that she wanted the person she liked to yell at her for hours and hours?!"

"Nobody went that far." Charlie scolded Natsunagi, sounding as if she

was genuinely worried. "You shouldn't say those things in front of men."
This was definitely the scene I'd least wanted to witness this year.

"I see. So you've had it rough for quite a long time, Kimizuka." Saikawa
gazed at me, getting the conversation back on topic. "If you had such an
unusual experience, why haven't you ever mentioned it to us?" Something
about it seemed to tug at the idol singer; she tilted her head. "I mean, your
stories are always pretty weak, you know. You should share the ones
about car chases and things first."

"Saikawa, when you give advice, try to do it without hurting people."
What if I stopped being able to speak in public because I was traumatized
by that comment? "I'm pretty sure you've always listened to me with a
smile."

"Oh, I was practicing being sweet for fans at handshake events!"

"I just learned something ugly about idols…"

Still, as her producer, if my noble sacrifice made the idol Yui-nya shine
brighter, maybe there was no greater joy.

…As her producer?

"Still, I didn't expect that." Natsunagi turned to me. She and Charlie
seemed to have wrapped up their comedy skit.

"What? You realized my side profile was unexpectedly attractive?"

"No, that wasn't unexpected; it happens all the time—er, no, I mean
'never,' or not."

Not? I don't really get what "not" means in this case.

"I meant that first story. The one about Danny Bryant. He doesn't seem
to be associated with you now, or… Hmm. I'm not sure how to phrase it."
Natsunagi put a finger to her chin, thinking. "Does that mean the apartment you live in now used to be Danny's place?" she asked, turning back
to me.

Saikawa and Charlie seemed curious about that, too. Like Natsunagi,
they gazed at me intently.

"If you had a bird's-eye view of us right now, it would look like I had a
harem." I smiled wryly, taking a sip of my extremely sweet coffee.

"That doesn't sound like you, Kimizuka."

"Yes, I second that."

For some reason, Charlie and Saikawa didn't seem happy about that.

"That bit about your side profile a minute ago, too. You don't usually act
narcissistic like that." Even Natsunagi was eyeing me dubiously.

Sheesh. When did they make such a detailed profile of me?

"You were trying to change the subject, weren't you?" Natsunagi leaned in, getting straight to the point.

I hadn't been trying to hide anything... But it was true that I didn't think my old stories were that interesting, and I'd hesitated a little.

It seems the high school girl, idol, and agent had all inherited the former Ace Detective's observational skills.

"And? It's the part that comes next that's important, right?" Charlie asked, urging me to continue.

I'd started sharing this story because we were talking about birthdays. As Charlie had guessed, the story would go on for a while: until *my birthday that one year*, on May 5. At the very least, it wouldn't end until we'd reached some sort of conclusion.

"Tell us a sidesplitting, hilarious story that will have us rolling in the aisles, Kimizuka!" Saikawa's eyes sparkled.

Raising the bar like that makes it a whole lot harder for me...but I guess that's nothing new, either.

We'd finished lunch, but there was still plenty of time before the next thing on our schedule. Figuring we'd stay here and talk for a while longer, I geared up to resume my story.

"In that case, I'll go get us more drinks!"

...Hey. *You were the one who wanted to hear it, Natsunagi*, I retorted in my mind as I watched her leave.

"...Um. Kimizuka? Would you come help me?" Natsunagi turned back, scratching at her cheek in embarrassment.

It appears my story was going to have to wait until we picked up those drinks.

Chapter 2

◆ April 28　Siesta

"See? What did I tell you? Just wander around town and you'll run into that kid, up to his ears in some incident or other."

I'd visited this police station just two days before. In one of its hallways, Fuubi Kase was smiling at me triumphantly for some reason. "He didn't just get pulled in this time, he was actually involved."

About an hour earlier, a murder had occurred in a mixed-use building. The victim was a man in his forties who ran a consumer finance company; he'd been stabbed in the chest and had died from blood loss. I'd seen Boy K. at the scene, holding a knife that appeared to be the murder weapon, and had called it in. From the look of the situation, he clearly knew something.

However, no matter what I'd asked him, he didn't respond. The only thing he'd told me was his name. He'd stayed silent in the police car on the way to the police station, too. And now here we were... In an interview room near the hall where Fuubi and I were talking, Boy K. was being questioned as a suspect.

"But he's not fourteen yet, is he? Under the laws of Japan, youth offenders can't be punished. You can't even conduct a criminal investigation on them, correct?"

"Right, which is why this isn't an investigation. It's just an *inquiry*. We've contacted the children's welfare center. Nobody's going to care if we talk to him until they come pick him up." Fuubi leaned back against the wall.

"Does Boy K. have any family? Aside from Danny Bryant, I mean."

"It's pretty late for that question, isn't it? You know he's on his own."

It seems she found out I'd infiltrated city hall. Not that it mattered.

"Geez. Who's the spy here? Even I didn't recognize you for a minute." I was blending into the scene in my disguise as a police officer. Fuubi shot me a look, then sighed.

"Then while I'm here, let me handle Boy K.'s questioning, too. You're having trouble with him, aren't you?"

From what I'd heard, even in the interview room, he still wasn't talking.

"The detective should stay out of this until we've got a closed circle mystery on our hands, don't you think?" Fuubi narrowed her eyes at me, clearly not happy with my suggestion.

"But I saw the crime scene up close."

"How am I supposed to explain it to the higher-ups?"

"Just get orders from above them." If the orders came from somebody who worked for the world itself, someone who vastly outranked a mere civil servant, then…

"As if those guys would lift a finger over a murder in this backwater."

"Then you can grant permission."

"Kid, you've been treating me like a handyman lately." Fuubi scratched her head irritably, but then, she said, "…Finish up in fifteen." She used her intercom to contact somebody.

Had she left this to me, even though she griped about it, because she'd seen time and time again how much trouble Boy K. was? Or was it because she knew I never backed down at times like this? Either way, I was grateful. It was my belief that if detectives and the police teamed up, the world's mystery novels could cut their page counts in half.

A little while after that, I was ready. Still in my police officer disguise, I stepped into the interview room where Boy K. waited. "We meet again, kid."

The room was cold and spare; except for the table and chairs in its center, it was empty. Boy K. was sitting in one of the chairs. He glanced at me, then looked down at his hands again.

He'd been wearing a jacket at the crime scene, but he'd undergone a body search and was now in a plain T-shirt. Although he still looked young, he had a rather melancholic expression. I would describe him as more mature than resigned.

"There are surveillance cameras in here, so people can see us," I said as I took a seat across the table from the boy. He still wouldn't meet my eyes. "So you don't have to worry, I won't use force to interrogate you illegally, and the 'right to remain silent' you've been exercising is still guaranteed. You also have the right to legal representation; if you need it, I can make the arrangements." At that point, Boy K. finally looked my way. "I'm definitely not your ally, but I'm not your enemy, either. I'm... Oh, of course, I haven't introduced myself yet, have I?"

Since I was disguised as a police officer, I was hesitant to use my code name or bynames. Instead, I held out my fake police notebook. "My name is Gekka. Gekka Shirogane."

The name stemmed from my actual hair color, and on the *gekka bijin*, or "moonlight beauty," a white flower that only bloomed at night.

"And your name is—Kimihiko Kimizuka, correct? What should I call you?" As I tried to establish a connection, I narrowed my focus to winning his trust.

I kept watching him steadily, and the boy finally caved. "Kimizuka or Kimihiko. Call me whatever you want."

"Thank you. Okay then, kid..."

"What, you're not using my name?"

That was a surprisingly snappy comeback. You'd never think he'd just killed a guy. Well, maybe he hadn't.

"Oh, I see. Did you want *your big sister here* to call you by your name?" My actual age might be one thing, but in terms of apparent age, I had ten years on him at the moment.

Boy K. looked away defiantly. "Don't treat me like a child. I'm an adult."

"Only kids ever say that."

"If you round up a bit, I'm hundred and sixty centimeters tall."

"It's all right. At your age, boys have sudden growth spurts." At present, he was a little shorter than average. Just a little. "They've told me a bit about you. I hear you're always getting caught up in crazy incidents?"

"...It's how I'm wired. Thanks to that, nobody comes near me."

"It sounds like you're really popular with the police, though." As I said it, I was thinking of the redheaded policewoman's aggrieved face.

"You said you were Ms. Gekka? *What are you trying to pull here?*" Boy K. glared at me, as if he were sizing me up. "Are you starting with random chitchat to get me to lower my guard? Is that your plan? You're a good negotiator." He didn't sound amused.

"You're not cute, are you, kid?"

"Nobody wants the police to think they're cute."

Really? That fiend of a policewoman might be one thing, but being doted on by me seemed like it would be more of a reward than anything else.

"If you insist, then: Let's get down to business." Fuubi had given me fifteen minutes. I couldn't really afford to take my time anyway. "So? What were you doing in a place like that?"

The room where I'd found Boy K. holding that knife had been a loan shark's office. Normally, a kid his age wouldn't have any opportunity to visit a place like that. If Boy K. had actually committed a murder there, what had brought him to the office in the first place?

After I asked him about it, Boy K.'s eyes widened slightly, as if I'd surprised him somehow. Not by my question, though—I'd shown him a note, positioning it so that the surveillance camera couldn't see it.

I'd like you to answer the questions I write down, not the ones I ask aloud. This message was written on the note.

I really did intend to solve this incident. However, my original goal, the real reason I'd been looking for Boy K., was something else. The boy pressed his lips together, carefully considering my intentions, and I stealthily showed him another note.

The boy's expression briefly changed. "...I dunno," he answered. He wasn't responding to my question of "what he'd been doing in a place like that." The second note had said, *Do you know a man named Danny Bryant?*

That was why I was sticking close to Boy K. If the children's welfare center took custody of him temporarily, I might lose this tenuous lead on Danny. A member of the Federation Government had entrusted me with this case, and she'd gone so far as to personally request it. Learning Danny Bryant's true identity would be highly significant for me as well.

"Did you stab that loan shark?"

I asked about the murder aloud, but my note read, *Do you know where Danny is?*

"......"

The boy didn't answer. However, from his earlier reaction, it was clear that he had some sort of connection to the man. I drew random strokes in my notepad, then held it out to the boy. "I've drawn a rough map of the crime scene, but there are a few things I can't remember about the layout. Can you fill those in?"

Now he could write down his answers to my real questions without arousing suspicion.

With a small sigh, the boy picked up the notepad. "Is this good enough?" I'd asked him where Danny Bryant was, and as his response, he'd written:

If you prove I'm innocent, I don't mind telling you where Danny's hiding.

"Sorry to keep you waiting. Let's continue on, shall we?" I'd temporarily stepped out of the interrogation room, then returned to face Boy K. again.

"I figured evidence that proved my innocence had turned up and I'd been acquitted." The boy shrugged and accepted the fact that I'd resumed my seat.

Was he so composed because he wasn't nervous anymore, or was it because he'd grown accustomed to these situations? Or—had that deal with me helped him decide where he stood? Whichever it was, it made it easier for me to work.

"I wanted to have our interview time extended a little. I stepped out to ask about that, and I've also had them temporarily shut off the surveillance cameras in here."

"I'm pretty sure you said something about how those cameras ensured my safety. You'd better not be planning to use a truth serum on me."

"Conversing in writing the whole time was going to be a pain, that's all. Besides, when I get serious, I don't waste time with trivialities."

"You're saying you've got an attack that could do more than break my skull?" Boy K.'s face tensed up, and he pushed his chair back.

"It destroys human dignity."

"That's not something a cop should be saying..."

I'm actually a detective, so it's not a problem.

"Still, now I can talk to you without worrying about anyone listening in."

What I needed to do now was prove Boy K.'s innocence, then get him to tell me where Danny Bryant was. It was simple enough.

The only thing I was concerned about was whether Boy K. was actually innocent. In terms of circumstantial evidence, he was the biggest suspect. I couldn't possibly bend the truth for the sake of my own objective.

I couldn't falsify the evidence so that it would work in our favor, and I couldn't file an insanity plea and have Boy K. declared not guilty. I had to prove he hadn't done it. That said, I couldn't rush this. I'd learned just recently that building a theory to fit a certain conclusion was about the dumbest move there was. Reining myself in, I took a different approach. "To start with, let's talk a little more about ourselves, shall we?"

The boy gave a thin smile. "Negotiating again?"

"I wouldn't go to so much trouble when you've already seen all my cards. It's just my policy. If I'm going to ask somebody to talk about themselves, I need to tell them something about myself as well."

Of course, that wasn't actually my policy. I wasn't even a cop. Right now, though, more than anything, I needed him to trust me.

"That's a weird thing to be so conscientious about," the boy said with a frankness I wasn't expecting. "Okay."

I told him a bit about where I'd been born and raised, what had made me decide to join the police force, and a few of the cases I'd been involved in previously. Naturally, most of what I said was a lie, but making all of it up would have made it less believable.

...And so I mixed in a few truths. For example, some of the "previous cases I'd been in charge of" were incidents I'd actually solved as a detective. As I told the boy about those, I mentioned that Danny Bryant was suspected of a certain theft, which was why I was pursuing him. As a matter of fact, I'd heard from Fuubi that Danny might have committed a few petty crimes like that.

"I see. Well, there are probably a zillion reasons for the cops to be after that guy." Boy K. smiled wryly. Then he began to tell me about Danny's character. He told me that the man had shown up one day, claiming to be a relative, and had taken him in, but just kept wandering off and hadn't really looked after him. That when he came home every so often, his clothes were always torn up for some reason, but he'd still be smiling cheerfully. And how he often acted as a sort of Robin Hood, which meant he made enemies easily. That Danny Bryant had constantly made Boy K.'s life difficult. He gave specific examples along with his explanation, too.

"Well, as I said, it's not like I'm with him all the time. We're each doing our own thing right now," he explained.

"And you say that while you were doing your own thing, you got dragged into this incident?"

"Yeah. It was a coincidence. When I went to that office for, uh, reasons," the boy said, lamenting his misfortune with exaggerated gestures. If that was true, I had to clear up this incident for him as quickly as possible.

I shifted the conversation back to the main topic. "In that case, let me ask you again. You said 'for reasons'; can we go into the specifics there?" I asked again, thinking he might tell me the truth now that we were on the same page. "It's not the sort of place kids usually visit."

"I'm living on my own, so I need money. I didn't think the place was that sketchy," he replied.

Boy K. had said that Danny Bryant wasn't actively taking care of him. Did that mean he wasn't making sure he had money, either?

"Let's say I believe you. You went to that office to borrow money, and then what happened?"

"When I got there, that yakuza guy was already bleeding on the floor."

"I see. Well, an ordinary person probably wouldn't believe that." As expected, he was planning to keep pleading innocent.

Now that I was facing Boy K., even I was having a hard time imagining him as the killer. It was the number of times he blinked, the movements of his eyes, the depth of his breathing; the sort of things I could see even without a polygraph.

What concerned me wasn't the question of whether he was lying or not, but the fact that Boy K. seemed to be gazing into the distance. It was as if he felt his battlefield was somewhere else.

"Then what about that knife you had?"

Even so, our objectives really had lined up. I searched the conversation for evidence that would prove Boy K.'s innocence.

"It was on the floor to begin with. I guessed it might be the murder weapon and picked it up without thinking; that's when you saw me."

"It doesn't really get worse than that, does it?"

Was this the power of Boy K.'s knack for getting dragged into things?

To summarize his story, he'd visited the consumer loan office to borrow money, discovered a yakuza member covered in blood, and carelessly picked up the knife used in the attack when I'd walked in and saw him.

It sounded like an improbably convenient testimony. He was the person in question, of course, so that was only to be expected. All that really mattered was objective proof.

Unfortunately, the office's security camera had been destroyed. That had to have been the work of the criminal. Either way, nothing that proved Boy K.'s innocence had been found yet.

"So you think the true culprit, the murderer, was somebody else."

"Yeah, *somebody* who stopped by before I did. Not that I can prove it," the boy said, laughing at himself. There were no security cameras near the alley where the building was located, and we hadn't yet figured out the foot traffic in that area.

At the moment, the police probably assumed the situation was something like this: Boy K., who was living in poverty, had unwisely gotten involved with a loan shark. Trouble had broken out at the office, and he'd killed his creditor. If Boy K. really was innocent, how were we going to turn this around?

"I'm used to being a suspect, though." The boy looked away, smiling a little. He seemed to have accepted his fate as inevitable, so I hesitated to compliment his courage.

"It's all right. Fortunately, I hear they've found multiple footprints at the crime scene. They haven't decided that you're the one who did it..."

Just then, Fuubi Kase contacted me on my intercom. The forensic results for the fingerprints on the murder weapon had come back. I listened intently.

"I see. All right, kid, we've got new information." I shared what I'd learned from Fuubi: "The only fingerprints on the knife used in the murder were yours."

"I see. I'm the perpetrator, then, huh."

"You certainly are."

We exchanged wry smiles.

It was too soon to give up, though. The real criminal might have worn gloves.

"You believe me?"

"I don't believe people." There were plenty of things more worthy of belief than people. "I want to know where Danny Bryant is. That means if you're not innocent, I'll have a problem on my hands."

"What if I actually am the murderer?" Boy K. asked without turning a hair.

True, I'd have to keep that possibility in mind as well. What if he was lying to me, made everything worse, and didn't even give me any information about Danny?

"Right. If so, rest assured you'll lose your dignity as a human being for all eternity." I smiled at him as calmly as possible, so he wouldn't be scared of me.

"…Seriously, Ms. Gekka, who are you?"

A detective, just a detective.

Not that I'm telling you that yet.

"That said, the fact of the matter is that this just seems weird. Could a kid really stab a yakuza member to death? I suspect there's someone else behind this."

The truth was still eluding me. But if I gathered a bit more information, or maybe revisited the crime scene armed with the facts I'd learned, I should be able to uncover something new there.

"Don't worry. I'm sure you'll be home in time for dinner."

Boy K.'s only response was a subdued "Yeah." He was gazing into the distance.

After that, having determined that I wouldn't be able to get anything else out of Boy K. at this point, I went to take a look at the evidence that had been collected from the crime scene.

In addition to the knife believed to be the murder weapon, there was a list of debtors and other related documents, the victim's cell phone, and the office computer. I set to work analyzing all of them. As usual, Fuubi grumbled, but I pointed out—again—that I'd taken over the search for Danny. She must have felt a little indebted to me, because she grudgingly gave her consent.

Before I knew it, while I was analyzing the new data I'd gleaned from the evidence, the sun had set. Even then, I still had a lot left to do. By the time I went to see Boy K., who'd been moved to the children's welfare center, it was quite late.

When I reached the center, I headed for the room where they were keeping him. I used my master key to unlock the door, and there was Boy K., lying on his side with his face to the wall.

"Good morning, kid," I whispered, putting my lips close to his ear.

"—! You scared me…" He bolted up after I'd startled him; maybe he'd been asleep.

"Do you have sensitive ears?"

"You wanna show me a person who doesn't?"

I don't. At the very least, having somebody blow into my ears doesn't faze me. …Although I doubt I'll have the opportunity to prove it.

"I'm sorry I'm so late. It's past dinnertime, isn't it?"

It had taken me longer than I thought to weigh the evidence, and I'd ended up breaking my promise.

"What time is it?" Flustered, the boy reached for his pocket, then realized they'd confiscated his smartphone.

"It's past eleven."

I wanted to let him have breakfast at his apartment tomorrow morning, at least. Come to think of it, I wondered if that bread was still good.

"...I see. Eleven." Boy K. wiped the sweat off his forehead and sighed. "So what do you need? From your face, I'm guessing my innocence hasn't been proven yet."

"It hasn't. I do think incidents should be solved at the scene of the crime, though. And so..."

"...What?" The boy cocked his head, mystified.

I extended my left hand to him. "Let's sneak out of here together."

With that, we ran away from the children's welfare center.

Fuubi Kase had nothing to do with this, of course. It was entirely my own decision.

"If she finds out, she might actually kill me this time. She's merciless." Remembering the battles I'd once fought with the Assassin, I pedaled faster.

Racing through the dark streets on a bicycle made me feel like I was wrapped in stars and the wind. It wasn't bad.

"Don't you usually use police cars for this sort of thing?" Boy K. whined from behind me. Unfortunately, I wasn't old enough to drive yet. Not that he knew that.

Well, I would if I had to. I'd like to learn how to drive a tank one of these days, just in case. You can never be too prepared. Especially when you're a detective.

"My first time riding double with somebody, and it's a cop. This sucks." Boy K. had simultaneously mocked himself and insulted me.

The kid might look resigned to his fate at all times, but he was cheeky.

"It's a good life experience, isn't it? It depends on how you look at it."

"And every way I look at this, it's bad. One classic teenage rite of passage, down the drain."

"I'm surprised you're interested in stuff like this. Your expression always looks so dead."

"Mind your own business. *Just because you're all dried up*, that doesn't mean other people— Whoa!"

I slammed on the brakes, and Boy K. hastily threw his arms around my waist, hanging on.

"Oh, sorry. A cat ran out in front of us. I couldn't help it."

"...! Ms. Gekka, maybe you don't look like it, but you're a little brat on the inside, aren't you?"

"An excellent question," I demurred, and we hurried to the scene of the crime.

About twenty minutes later...

"Okay, go on in. Just try not to leave fingerprints, and don't move things."

When we reached the mixed-use building, we crossed the police tape, then stepped into the consumer loan office where the incident had happened.

Wearing gloves, I flipped on the light switch. No one was there. The corpse had been taken away, of course, and nobody was around except Boy K. and me.

"And? Why bring me here?" The kid stayed near the door, without venturing any farther into the room. An unsurprising decision at the scene of a murder.

"I thought you might notice something new if you took another look at the crime scene. Come here." When I beckoned him, the boy steeled himself and came in. "The stars are very clear tonight, aren't they?" I said, looking at them through the big window.

"Is that a new pickup line?"

"Unfortunately, I'm only interested in older men." Wait, this isn't the conversation we should be having. "That curtain was open, wasn't it?"

The boy looked a little perplexed, as if he wasn't sure what I was getting at.

"When I first came here this afternoon, that curtain was open. If this murder was premeditated, that would have been really careless of the murderer, don't you think?"

"...Oh, actually, yeah. Normally you'd close the curtains so people wouldn't see."

"Right. So I think this was a crime of passion."

As a matter of fact, a staff member from this office was actually a witness: the man with the shaved head who'd almost run into me. The killer had been careless. I couldn't believe they'd had the murder planned out from the beginning.

"Yeah, but it's not like every murderer in the world tries to commit the perfect crime. Maybe whoever it was had an intense grudge against the victim and wanted to kill him so badly he didn't care whether people found out. The guy who got killed would've had a lot of enemies," Boy K. said.

Yes, in his line of work, he'd probably had a lot of people out for his blood.

"Still, the suspect is on the run. That means they didn't want their crime to be discovered."

That would still have been true even if Boy K. had been responsible, since he was denying the crime. Either way, our culprit wanted to run from the murder they'd spontaneously committed.

"I see. I guess the security camera was broken, huh."

"Right. And the fingerprints were wiped off the weapon."

"If we assume the criminal isn't me, anyway," the boy said, shrugging.

We weren't "assuming" anymore, though. I was sure that whoever had erased the proof was the true culprit.

"This was a place of business, no matter how unscrupulous it was. As such, I thought they'd have a list of scheduled visits. I checked into it."

"...! The computer, huh?" Boy K. snapped his fingers, as if it suddenly made sense.

"Good job remembering that. It isn't even here now."

"...Yeah. They probably took it in as evidence."

Should I compliment him on his familiarity with incidents like this?

"So what did you find? Was anybody besides me scheduled to visit today?"

"I looked at the schedule, but unfortunately, there weren't any appointments."

When I told him the other days had been full, Boy K. looked away. "Bad luck," he said regretfully.

"In exchange, though, I got this." I took certain documents out of the bag I'd brought along. "They're written debt acknowledgments from the borrowers. The due dates are on here as well. If one of these matched up, I thought we might have a likely suspect, but..."

"But there was nobody suspicious there, either, huh?" The kid finished my sentence for me.

"Right. Not in the office's *physical files*." From the boy's reaction, he hadn't been expecting that. "The borrowers' data was on the computer as well. Technically, part of it had been deleted—but I recovered it."

Boy K. listened to me in silence.

"I noticed data seemed to be missing from several places, including the scheduling tool. It took time, but when I restored the deleted data, a certain borrower came up. Not only that, but strangely, his was the only name not on the debtor list in the office."

It almost seemed like an attempt to let that borrower slip away from the crime scene. I didn't know whether he'd been the one who'd destroyed the evidence or whether he'd had help.

"Then you think the borrower who disappeared is the culprit?" Boy K. looked away; his expression was grim.

"I thought there was a good possibility. I called the phone number that was in the recovered data, but naturally, no one answered. However..." The boy looked at me. "As a matter of fact, you've already been released, kid. In exchange, a warrant's been issued for that borrower."

"...! Is there any definite proof?" Boy K. took a step closer to me; he seemed anxious.

"You're asking me that? You're finally being cleared of a false charge."

"......"

"Is there a reason you don't want him to be caught?"

"......"

If someone was protecting the borrower who was considered the real culprit...

If that someone was this boy, Kimihiko Kimizuka...

Then who was he trying to protect?

"—Hey, what are you two doing?"

Just then, a frustrated-sounding voice echoed through the crime scene. Our escape had been discovered.

"I'm sorry. I wanted to do a little nighttime cycling."

Fuubi Kase had come running with several police officers. I gave her an exaggerated wink, but it seemed to rub her the wrong way. "First you shove work onto people, then you pull selfish crap like this..." She shot me a murderous look.

"I didn't force it onto you. I'm relying on you."

"Ha! You always were a glib talker if nothing else."

How rude. My sniping skills are pretty decent, too.

"Let's cut to the chase, then."

Now it was time to solve the case. There were two of us, a detective and a police officer, so we'd wrap this up twice as fast.

"Let's clear this up, starting with the false charge on this kid," I said.

Fuubi returned my look wordlessly, agreeing to let me have the floor for now. Boy K. also stayed where he was. He watched me steadily, waiting to see what I'd do.

"First, let me preface this by saying I never thought the boy committed the murder in the first place. He had no motive for doing something that outrageous."

In the interview room, Boy K. had said something like "I visited that place for the first time." From what I'd seen of the loan office's list of customers, he'd been telling the truth. Coming up with a reason for a middle-school boy to kill a yakuza member he'd just met was nearly impossible.

"We've got material evidence, though." Fuubi interrupted earlier than I'd thought she would. She probably meant the fingerprints on the knife. "You can't just rely on motives. There's no telling what any human is thinking anyway. Objective evidence is the only thing you can trust," she said, glaring at Boy K.

"Ms. Fuubi, I figured you'd still be suspecting me."

"Ha! See, I never trusted you in the first place. The issue's more basic than whether I suspect you or not."

Boy K. and Fuubi exchanged glares.

"I sure miss that laidback police station chief."

"Now that he doesn't have to deal with you anymore, I bet he's kicking back and playing Go on the veranda with his grandkids."

…If I let these two get started, they'd probably keep fighting forever. I got us back on topic. "Yes, the forensic results showed the kid's fingerprints are on the knife." When I spoke again, both the boy and Fuubi looked my way. "That doesn't prove he actually committed the murder."

Fuubi was a police officer; she had to know this already.

"I saw the aftermath of the crime up close, and there wasn't a drop of blood on the boy's skin or clothes. It's impossible to believe that he'd just stabbed somebody."

When he'd stood there holding the knife, his profile had seemed melancholy and resigned. However, for some reason—he'd struck me as beautiful.

Well, that was just my subjective impression, but still. If he'd stabbed someone, it was very unlikely that he wouldn't have any blood on him. Therefore, as Boy K. had said, it seemed probable that he'd just picked up the murder weapon and had gotten his fingerprints on it then.

"And one more thing. The kid is *just a little too short* to have killed the victim."

Boy K. was about a hundred and sixty centimeters tall. The victim had been a big man, over a hundred and ninety centimeters, but he'd been stabbed in the chest.

Of course, even with a thirty-centimeter height difference, it wouldn't have been impossible for the boy's hand to reach the victim's chest. If he'd held the knife in a reverse grip and raised his arm high, then brought it down, even he could have performed the stabbing without trouble.

However, from examining the stab wound, we knew that the knife had been held nearly horizontally. If a hundred-and-sixty-centimeter-tall boy had stabbed someone who was thirty centimeters taller than him, it wouldn't have left the wound it did.

"So if I hadn't gone and touched the knife, I never even would have been a suspect?" The boy laughed at himself. "It's like I'm cursed. I get dragged into crap like this every time."

"Yes, I couldn't agree more," I said, sincerely sympathizing with the boy's remark. "Because of your predisposition, you keep encountering situations like this one. However, *just this once, you were truly careless.*"

The boy watched me silently.

"You're used to this sort of incident. They really should be routine for you. And yet you picked up that knife. Why?"

He had to have known that touching the weapon would make him a suspect. Boy K. should have understood that better than anyone... "You knew this would happen all along. You picked up the knife on purpose, didn't you?" In doing so, he had the police focus their attention on him as the prime suspect. He'd had all of us in the palm of his hand.

"Why would I do that?" Boy K. cocked his head and smiled, but it wasn't real.

"In order to protect someone."

Someone. The real killer.

Boy K. had kept insisting he was innocent, and yet he'd intentionally done something that would make him a suspect.

"Someone? Who would that even be? I'm always alone. You know that."

Indeed, we had talked about that at the station. Boy K. had no friends. I'd done some independent investigation, and from what I'd found, he had neither parents nor siblings. That meant there was no one who he would risk his life for. —Was there?

"Gekka," he said, dropping the "Ms." "You're saying the person who visited the office before I did is the criminal, right? Then what are they to me? Are they a friend who's so close I'd take a murder rap for them? Are they family? Or—"

I made eye contact with Fuubi. From here on out, this was her job.

"No. The real perpetrator is a total stranger to you."

Oh. Really?

I hadn't known that until she said it. I'd thought *the other possibility* had a higher chance, but maybe the truth tends to work that way.

"The suspect's a man in his forties who ran up a big debt with this office. His name is—"

Fuubi gave a name that matched one of the people on the list of customers. The name was the one I'd expected, at least.

"A minute ago, he called and confessed to the crime. His loan was due today, but he hadn't been able to get the money together. He'd gone to the office to ask them to wait, and negotiations broke down. The victim pulled a knife on him as a threat, they struggled, and we all know how that ended up. Whether or not they accept it as legitimate self-defense depends on how good his lawyer is." Fuubi sighed.

As incidents went, it was a really common one. The odd part was what came next.

"Then right after the incident, you happened to stop by the scene. For some reason, you took responsibility for the crime, and the suspect fled."

In other words, Boy K. had taken the fall for a murder committed by a stranger he'd just met.

"I took on a crime for some guy I don't even know? What would I get out of that?" The boy sounded shocked. It was a perfectly natural question.

But right after that...

"Still, I guess my job's over now." Boy K.'s expression softened just a little; he seemed relieved. It was as if he felt there was no point in resisting any longer. Either that, or he'd already done what he'd set out to do. "Yeah, it's just like you said. I was covering for the real criminal."

"Why? You had nothing to do with this."

Now it was my turn to ask questions. If the person Boy K. was protecting had been *the man I was pursuing*, I would have understood his actions. This time, though, it had been the other possibility.

"When I ran into the culprit here, he told me something. He seemed to be panicking." The boy started to speak, quietly. "He said his daughter was having surgery soon. She had a severe illness, and this was a major surgery that would determine whether she'll live or die. If he got caught, he might never see her again—so he begged me to let him go, *just for today*, so he could see his daughter. That's why I pretended I was the criminal for a day," Boy K. said. He looked out the window at the night sky.

"I see. So you wanted to give him one last day with his daughter..."

It made sense. All the pieces fell into place.

Although he'd been trying to protect the criminal, several footprints had been left at the scene, the computer's data hadn't been completely erased, and the issue involving the height difference hadn't been resolved. I'd chalked all those things up to Boy K.'s inexperience.

At the same time, I'd thought maybe that was inevitable. No ordinary middle schooler could completely destroy evidence that easily.

But I'd been wrong. He'd left patchy evidence simply because he'd only had to play this role for a day. He hadn't left any proof that would truly implicate him; he'd stuck to being a twenty-four-hour-long scapegoat.

Wow. He's even smarter than I imagined. That had to be a byproduct of the experiences his predisposition had put him through.

"If the criminal confessed, though, then he already saw his daughter. That means my job is done."

The boy wasn't smiling. He only looked a little tired, as if the fact that he'd finished helping someone was sinking in.

I'll say it again: He was clever. Really clever.

At the same time, I had to admit he was naive.

"Even if it was just for a day, why take such a huge risk?"

The boy had made this sacrifice in an attempt to grant someone's wish, but had he gained anything worth the dangers?

"This guy told me before—he said to at least help the people in front of me."

"The only people who can say things like that are the ones with enough resolution and strength to save anyone. That isn't you."

"—Except I did pull it off this time. But, yeah, helping a criminal avoid arrest is a crime. I'll take the rap for that one."

"Did you really think that was the right thing to do? Overlooking a crime? Really?"

"...I don't know. I think that's probably why I picked up that knife before I realized what I was doing: because I didn't know the answer."

A father had saddled himself with debt, committed a crime, and had wanted to see his daughter one more time—the boy didn't have a family, so he didn't understand why. He told us so, as if he were talking to himself.

"Yeah, you really are a damn brat." Fuubi glared at the boy. Her eyes were full of disgust—cold as ice, really. "Here, I'll tell you that answer: There never was any surgery."

"...!" The kid's eyes widened. "That's...not even... He didn't look like he was lying..."

"The killer probably wasn't the one who lied. Isn't that right?" I looked at Fuubi.

She nodded. "The liar was the yakuza who got bumped off. He said he'd use his connections to hook the guy up with a doctor who'd take on his daughter's tough surgery; then he gave him a high-interest loan, telling him it was his fee for the introduction. Except he never had any connections, and the scheduled surgery was a fake."

Fuubi's investigations had uncovered the truth, and her lips were pressed together in a thin line, her face expressionless. There was no outward change from her usual demeanor, but she was definitely furious on the inside. That was the impression I got, anyway.

"He told a lie like that, just to swindle him out of money...?" That seemed to shock the boy; he bit his lip hard.

The criminal had probably also learned everything immediately before the incident, which was why he'd finally turned himself in.

"Listen, kid…"

What should I say at a time like this? Comforting someone wasn't part of a detective's job. I knew that. But even so.

"You can't look for the answers you want in other people." Those words weren't based in anything I'd been thinking. They'd just left my mouth before I knew them. "If you want an answer, you have to find it on your own."

I was sure that was true for me as well. I was speaking both to the boy and to myself.

I was missing some memories. I had an enemy I needed to defeat. There were things I had to reclaim. And so I…

"It's all right. Leave it to me." When he heard that, the boy finally looked up. "I know where to find a skilled doctor. He'll save the life of the girl you and the culprit were trying to protect."

"…Really?"

Yes, because he was born to save others.

And so, for now…

"Just relax and impose on the officer here for a while."

Boy K. seemed like I caught him off guard. Then he gave a little laugh, acknowledging his defeat.

◇ April 29   Kimihiko Kimizuka

That day, when I finally dragged myself home, I found a guy lounging around the Japanese-style room as if he owned the place. "Hey, you're late. Does your school have class for nine periods? Japanese students must work real hard." The man glanced at me; he was smirking. He knew roughly what I'd been going through before I made it home, and he was still acting this way.

"I got pulled into a little trouble, as usual."

"I see. You could have had Danny Bryant the handyman here clear that up for you, you know."

"I figured you'd charge some ridiculous retaining fee, so I decided not to," I said bluntly.

Danny gave a dry, cheerful laugh.

Still, who'd have thought I'd get pulled into another incident right on the heels of that car chase two days ago? Heaving a big sigh, I lowered my battered self onto a floor cushion.

There was pizza on the low table; Danny had probably ordered it. There was only a quarter left.

"Smoking too much will take years off your life," I warned Danny, pouring myself a glass of soda. On the other side of the table, he was about to light a cigarette.

"Oh-ho. You're saying you want me to live for a long time?"

"It was just a general comment. I won't say it again."

"Ha-ha! It may be poison for the body, but it's medicine for the spirit, see." Joking around, Danny exhaled a generous puff of white smoke. The guy was always so easygoing; even he needed medicine for his spirit sometimes? ...I couldn't ask him, so the question was pointless to consider.

"Once you're done eating, we're headed to work." Still smoking, Danny pulled a document out of his beat-up bag. It was a long list of names and phone numbers.

"Just call all the numbers on that list."

Every so often, Danny would come back to the apartment and have me help out with jobs like this. He paid me for it, and I'd been saving up so that I could live on my own someday, but...

"This isn't fraud, right?" I asked, suddenly uneasy.

Exactly what kind of list had Danny brought me? He'd better not be planning to make me call people and say, "I messed up and embezzled company funds..." or something.

"Ha-ha. Your voice is a bit too high for impersonating a blundering office worker."

He was right. My voice wasn't done changing yet.

"Then what do you want me to do?"

"Just call those numbers and ask if their kid can come over and play."

"That makes no sense..." *What is this, a volunteer effort to help me make friends?* "How does this job get us any money?"

"The world isn't that simple," Danny lectured me. "It's like they say: 'When the wind blows, barrel makers get rich.' At the very end, when everything comes full circle, sometimes the results aren't what you'd expect."

He'd told me he was from America, but he knew his Japanese proverbs pretty well.

Was he trying to tell me that it would make sense to me someday? I felt like the saying he'd used to illustrate that didn't quite convey what he wanted, but whatever.

"You could also call it the butterfly effect. When a butterfly flaps its wings in your backyard, later on, after all sorts of twists and turns, it'll cause a hurricane in some distant country." Danny set a bottle of beer on the table and gazed out the window; the curtains were open.

There was a magnificent full moon tonight.

"That said, it's a fact that I'm short on money. I'll have to do a big job soon."

Apparently, the job he'd just brought in really wasn't going to earn us any money. Even so, Danny gave a big yawn. He didn't seem stressed.

"If you're short on money, then don't go out and buy stuff you don't need. How much did that picture cost?" I pointed at a landscape painting by an unknown artist that Danny had brought back one time as a "souvenir."

It was a bad habit of his. There were lots of similar works of art in the apartment.

"Oh, I happened to run into a young woman who said she was an art dealer on the street near here. It sounded like she was having a hard time making ends meet, so I bought it at her asking price."

...So he'd actually picked up his "souvenir" in town? Geez.

"You sure she didn't just trick you?"

"What? Is it not okay to get tricked?" With a straight face, Danny tilted his head. "Even if I was, the woman who was down on her luck was able to earn money. Now she'll be able to have bread and yogurt for breakfast tomorrow. Was what I did wrong, in human terms? If you don't at least help the people you can see, what's the point?" he asked glibly. He said that all the time.

Even if he had been scammed, his loss would be someone else's gain. It wasn't as if happiness was lost; the wealth had just shifted from the haves to the have-nots. Even if someone called that hypocrisy, Danny would probably stick to his convictions.

"You mean getting conned is better than doubting somebody, huh? That sounds like you."

I didn't actually know what sort of person Danny was. It wasn't like we'd been together constantly for the past few years. But that was sort of how I viewed him.

"You still have a ton of growing up to do, kid."

I thought I'd wrapped the conversation up nicely, but for some reason, Danny got mad at me. Why, though?

"'Even if you get conned, it's better than doubting somebody'? Ha-ha. Okay then: Say you fall for a scam, and they take your money. Where does that money go? For the most part, fraudsters like that have a boss. Your stolen money ends up funding more organized crime. Could you still say that line then?" Danny asked.

Was it fair to say that getting scammed was worth it as long as it made someone happy?

"Falling for a grift is basically committing a crime," Danny concluded, staring at me sternly.

"Say that in the first place, then."

Danny had a point, though. "Getting conned is better than doubting somebody" really might be just a shallow idea that sounded nice.

"...Wait, but that makes it worse. Why'd you buy that painting?" He had to have known it could've been a scam, right?

"Because sometimes I want to prioritize pretty platitudes, even if it means committing a crime. After all, I'm human." Danny laughed. "Besides, if you ever need money, try putting that painting up for sale. I bet it'll save your butt."

Sheesh. So was the painting worth anything or not?

"Everything is case-by-case. The world's not just black and white. There's pink and gold and sapphire, too. Sometimes you'll have to use your eyes and ears, experience, and sixth sense to make a call on something," Danny muttered, more to himself than to me. Then he drained the rest of his beer, drinking it right from the bottle.

What he was saying sounded like a bit too much to ask from a kid like me. "The one thing I'm sure of here seems to be that you have no money."

"Ha-ha! You got that right." Danny laughed, then lay down on the floor. The beer might have been getting to him; he closed his eyes.

Maybe he really was going to sleep here tonight.

"So, since I've got no money, I can't pay your wages for a while."

"Um, they're going to shut off the water soon."

"And that's when you start drinkin'."

This guy is an idiot.

Danny was falling asleep, so I placed a thin blanket over him.

"There may be somebody after me again."

Danny murmured out of nowhere. His eyes were still closed.

He probably meant somebody besides the guys from the car chase.

"If you run into them…"

"I'll say I don't know where you are. Right?"

That was our promise.

"Yup. If somebody sketchy makes contact with you, go ahead and lie. That's how you'll get ahead in life," Danny advised me from his spot on the floor.

"You're telling me to become a con man?"

"Given your little predisposition there, if you're going to take on the cops and detectives, you're gonna have to be either a con man or a phantom thief."

"…So we're assuming I'll be dealing with cops and detectives, huh?"

"Ha-ha. It's your destiny. Suck it up."

If that were true, being a corporate drone who had to work around the clock would be a hundred times better.

"Oh, right. While I'm at it, I need to tell you one more thing."

Sheesh. I wish he'd decide whether he's going to sleep or continue talking.

"I'll be traveling again for a while. Watch the place while I'm gone."

"You don't need to tell me to watch the place by now. Where are you going?" I wasn't that interested, but the conversation was naturally heading in that direction.

"To see the Sea of Japan," Danny responded.

It was a pretty abstract answer, but if that was what he wanted, I guessed he'd be headed for the Hokuriku region.

That said, sightseeing was never Danny's main objective.

"This job's going to be kind of a hairy one. Don't worry about it, though; you just do your thing and keep getting pulled into bank robberies and bus hijacks."

Danny had disappeared on a moment's notice before, multiple times. He'd never lived in this apartment regularly. I just responded with a brief "I see."

"I'm going to do what I want. That's what I've always done, and I don't intend to stop now. So do whatever you want, too. You're not even my kid, and I'm not your dad. I've got no plans to tie you down."

I seemed to recall him saying something about being my father figure just a little while back, but apparently, that had been an offhand joke.

"That's what humans are like, though, right? Yeah, and that's how it should be. If I gave you any big-headed lectures today, yesterday, or in the past, just ignore 'em all. If you start listening to a rapper tomorrow and decide to make life choices based on the lyrics, then that's one way to live."

"Your convictions are about as firm as a marshmallow."

"Ha-ha! Well, if your convictions are as solid as iron, you'll have one hell of a time when they break." Resting his head on his arm, Danny smiled with his eyes closed. "The stuff you like is a series of coincidences, and the way you live should be, too. I told you to become a phantom thief or a con man, but you could be a police officer or a detective if you want. The important thing is what you personally want to do in the moment, and that's it."

"Normally only kids can get away with that kind of selfishness."

"Ha-ha! Yeah, maybe. Maybe so." Danny sat up, gazing at me with a small smile. "But don't forget: You are a kid. Pester more, want more, be self-centered. That's a special privilege reserved for those your age. It's the cost of not smoking or drinking."

"...Even if I cause trouble for other people, you mean?"

"Humans cause trouble for someone or other just by being alive, whether they want to or not. If you can't live clean, then at least live selfishly before you die. That's what being human is all about."

As Danny Bryant said that, his eyes seemed to be fixed on a view I couldn't see.

◆ April 30   Siesta

"I see. So the kid was acquitted."

In the antique shop where I'd been living since I arrived in Japan, I was swaying back and forth in a rocking chair and talking to Fuubi on the phone.

It was a little past two in the afternoon. Not one person had come in since I'd opened the shop, and the soft afternoon sunlight that streamed in was making me deliciously drowsy.

"Yeah, it's a cryin' shame." Fuubi sighed heavily. "I didn't get to arrest the damn brat this time, either," she said. It was an uncharacteristically blatant complaint.

"I think you dislike him a bit too much, don't you? It's not like he killed your parents."

"If that was his only offense, he wouldn't get under my skin like this."

While I'd love to think that had been an *assassin joke*, if he caused incidents as nasty as that one on a frequent basis, her reaction might actually be warranted.

Take that murder at the consumer loan office the day before yesterday, for example. At first, Boy K. had been a suspect, but we'd found out that he was only covering for the real murderer, due to some convoluted circumstances. That would have counted as helping a criminal avoid arrest, and he would have been charged with that instead.

However, that night, the criminal had confessed. When the details of the incident came to light, we'd learned that the man responsible had broken the office's security camera and erased the data on the computer. Meaning all Boy K. had done was *accidentally* pick up a knife from the floor. We'd had no way to charge him for a crime, and no evidence to use against him. In that sense, that lone kid had beaten both the police and the detective hollow.

"He got you, too, huh," Fuubi said, sympathizing with me. "You thought the criminal he was covering for might be Danny Bryant, right?"

She was right. At first, I'd thought that was the most likely possibility. Boy K. had no friends or family, so if he was going to voluntarily take the fall for someone, I'd thought it might be the man claiming to be his relative.

However, I'd been wrong. Boy K. had been covering for a man he'd just met. He seemed to be at a crossroads, wrestling with a major question, and he'd done what he did in an attempt to find the answer to it.

"It's true that I couldn't find Danny this time, but I think I'll make progress before too long," I said. That wasn't my intuition talking. I felt quite certain about it.

"Oh-ho. Do you have any grounds for that statement?"

Yes, I sure did. However, the surest thing was—

"Sorry, it looks like I've got a customer. See you," I told Fuubi, then hung up. Right after that...

"You look a lot different than the last time I saw you, Gekka Shirogane."

The boy, Kimihiko Kimizuka, was the first customer of the day. He gazed at me dubiously. My class change from police officer to antique store owner seemed to have perplexed him to no end.

"I thought you'd come."

I invited him to come inside and take a load off in front of the counter.

Boy K. sat down in an antique chair and was staring at me so hard it seemed like he might burn a hole in my face. He'd been carrying a bundle under his arm and set it down gently on the floor. "Let me ask you one more time: Are you really Gekka?"

Two nights ago, after the incident had technically been resolved, I'd told Boy K. this address and my actual identity. Except...

"I notice you've casually dropped the 'Ms.' when you address me."

I still looked like a woman in my twenties, but he'd dispensed with the formalities.

"I spent a while mulling things over, and not being so formal with you just felt like right thing to do."

The kid was shockingly self-centered. Well, considering our actual ages, it was fine if he wanted to skip the honorifics. Even so, it was a pretty unique way of shrinking interpersonal distance.

Since he didn't have any friends, I'd assumed he'd struggle with conversation, but he was the opposite: He stuck to his guns no matter who he was talking to. It might be a little similar to the way I lived.

"That aside, that's one heck of a transformation. How did you do that?" The boy stared at my toes, then his eyes gradually traveled up.

"You focused on my chest for quite a while."

"...I bet you were imagining that."

"Kid, do you know what the world calls relationships between a woman and a younger boy?"

"Anyway, let's get down to business!"

His childlike flushed cheeks seemed like the real deal. If I picked on him anymore, though, I'd end up stalling the conversation, so I controlled myself.

"I'm a hero who lives in the criminal underworld: *The Fiend with Twenty Faces*."

Once again, I told him my true identity that I'd revealed to him two nights ago.

"...But everything about you is different from before. Even your height."

"I'm wearing a special mask and using shoe lifts to add to my height."

"What's your real age?"

"Never ask women that question."

I gave a thin smile, and the boy stared dully back in an open display of boredom. Yes, that's a good face.

"Come to think of it, there was something I wanted to ask you, kid." There was one thing I hadn't checked on after the incident the other day. "You said you got dragged into that mess because you went to the consumer loan office to borrow money. That was a lie, wasn't it?"

The boy blinked. "You figured that out, too, huh?" He smiled thinly. I couldn't visualize someone as clever as him to be visiting a place like that without knowing what it was.

"Were you just passing by? Or did they call you into the office because you had some previous history with them?" With his knack for getting dragged into trouble, that was plausible.

"...The latter. Back then, I thought being honest about that might have implicated me."

I see. Yes, that really might have tipped the scales. Even if the truth had been bound to come out sooner or later.

"There was no record of any contact with you in the call history on the victim's cell phone, though."

Naturally, I'd assumed some of it might have been erased, so I had restored that data as well.

"Right, because he called this phone instead." The boy took out a cell phone and showed it to me. "It's one Danny was using. He had several that he used for different purposes; this is one of the phones he left behind."

He'd left it behind—meaning Danny Bryant really wasn't anywhere near Boy K. at the moment.

"And is *that* why you came here today?"

Now we were getting to the point. My eyes traveled to the square, cloth-wrapped bundle that Boy K. had brought in.

"I came to pay back that favor today." The boy undid the cloth, revealing several works of art. They were all pastoral landscapes. "These are all the paintings Danny had."

True, I had heard that Danny Bryant had collected antiques and art before his disappearance. That was why I was pretending to run an antique shop.

"You're saying that these paintings show where he is?"

"That's my suspicion, anyway."

My deal with Boy K. had been that, in exchange for proving his innocence, he'd tell me where Danny was.

"I actually don't know where he is right now, either, so I brought these instead."

"So you're looking for him, too?"

"Yeah. In other words, our interests are aligned." But as he said it, the boy averted his eyes.

My intuition told me he was hiding something. There was no sense in pointing that out right now, though. Besides... "Why would these landscape paintings show us where Danny is?"

There had to still be information I could get out of the boy. It should be all right to let him do as he pleased for a little while.

"Danny said that if he disappeared, I should sell them. He might just have meant for me to use the money to cover my living expenses, but I... I couldn't see it that way." He met my eyes as he spoke. For some reason, he really did seem to think these oil paintings were connected to Danny Bryant's whereabouts.

Once again, I studied the paintings the boy had brought in. *The paintings I'd just seen at his apartment two days ago.*

"I see."

The boy had probably brought these without knowing I'd broken in and seen them already. However, now that they were here, the pictures took on a different significance. Boy K., who had spent several years building a relationship with Danny Bryant, was convinced that there was more to them.

"I thought you might know something about what they meant."

Boy K. must still have a secret he couldn't tell me. He was hiding something. But I could tell there was something he wanted to know, too. He was looking for answers. Was this about the familial love he'd mentioned that night at the crime scene? Or was it Danny Bryant's whereabouts? —Either way...

"Client requests must be granted," I said, reminding myself.

That was the beginning of our journey in search of Danny Bryant.

A certain girl's tale 2

When I'd read up to that point, I looked up. "So this was your real first meeting with Kimihiko, Mistress Siesta."

Mistress Siesta was still sleeping peacefully on the bed. I wondered what she was dreaming about. Was it Kimihiko, whom she was still calling "Boy K." at this point in her journal? He appeared and vanished unexpectedly at crime scenes, so I imagined it wouldn't be odd for him to turn up in others' dreams as well.

"What did you think of Kimihiko back then, Mistress Siesta?"

I knew she wouldn't answer, but I asked her anyway.

From Mistress Siesta's journal, the impression I got of Kimihiko was that he was a very clever and interesting person. Or maybe she'd thought of him as a mysterious boy who was rather lonely and fragile. A boy with many secrets as well.

Either way, she probably hadn't been thinking of making him her assistant yet…

Still, the environment in which he'd been raised and his way of connecting with others were similar to hers. Mistress Siesta must have found him intriguing.

Meanwhile, what had Kimihiko thought of Mistress Siesta—or rather, the mysterious Fiend with Twenty Faces? I didn't have access to his journal, so I had no way of knowing. In any case, their interests were compatible, and they were about to embark on a journey in pursuit of Danny Bryant.

Had this been the first time Mistress Siesta and Kimihiko worked together? The world's Ace Detective and her trouble-magnet assistant—if those two were together, something was bound to happen. Mistress Siesta must have known that as well.

And perhaps she had already suspected *a certain truth* at this point in time…but maybe I was jumping to conclusions there.

In any case, the tale of those past few days—which I was about to resume reading—hadn't been pointless for the two of them.

After all, their three-year adventure had its beginnings here.

Chapter 3

◆ May 1   Siesta

I was aware that I was dreaming.

"Seed, what are you trying to accomplish?"

After all, the one who said that was *the past me*, while *the current me* was gazing at this scene, floating in midair.

A year ago, I'd chased and chased a certain enemy until I'd reached a vast limestone cavern. The great evil lurked there, too deep for sunlight to reach. Multiple writhing tentacles sprouted from the white-haired young man's back.

"Something humanity could never understand," the enemy of the world said.

He'd already defeated me. I was no match for him, in wits or in strength. I might as well have been an infant as far as he was concerned, and I knelt before him, bleeding.

This is a dream, I remembered.

This was the memory of a defeat—of humiliation I'd lived through a year ago.

"Someday, I swear I'll defeat you."

At the time, it was all I could do to make that declaration. For some reason, the enemy hadn't finished me off.

"Will you sacrifice your companions again?" Seed asked, even though I'd gone into this battle alone. Something similar to disappointment surfaced in his eyes. He transformed, shape-shifting through a series of young boys and girls, but still, he didn't attack.

"...What are you trying to say?"

The last shape Seed assumed belonged to a girl with black hair and red eyes. He didn't answer my question. I didn't recognize the girl. After he'd watched my reaction, he faded and vanished, like Chameleon.

"Companions? I don't have…"

I was missing memories of a certain time period.

If what the enemy was saying was true, had I stood by and watched my companions die, even if I no longer knew it?

At this point, those memories had vanished over the horizon.

What had I done in the past? What had I lost?

I… I was—

"_____!"

The alarm echoed through the room, pulling me out of the dream.

Even though it wasn't summer, my forehead and neck were covered in sweat, and my drenched pajamas clung to my skin. As I took several deep breaths, I sat up and reached for the phone by my pillow.

"…Somebody's calling?"

I'd thought it was my alarm, but the phone had been ringing. The name on the display was—Kimihiko Kimizuka.

Oh, right—we'd arranged to meet up this afternoon.

I checked the time. It was 2 PM. We'd planned to meet at one o'clock, but apparently, that had been a bit too early for me.

"Sorry to keep you waiting. Have you been here long?"

An hour later, I spotted a familiar silhouette at our designated meeting spot in front of the train station and called out to him.

"People who are five minutes late could say that, but you're two hours late. Who the heck do you think you—"

Grumbling, Boy K.—Kimihiko Kimizuka—turned around.

"…………"

However, as soon as he saw me, he averted his eyes.

"The Fiend with Twenty Faces goes through disguises like nobody's business."

I wasn't the police officer or the antique shop manager today. I wore a new mask and costume.

"Since I'm not on duty, I went with a casual outfit. What do you think?" I lifted my skirt slightly. Granted, his initial reaction had already clued me in.

"It's a bit too short. Also, sweaters make, um, certain things…more obvious," the kid mumbled, still focused on some point across the station.

"I thought I'd show you that the Fiend with Twenty Faces can change her face, her voice, and her cup size at will."

"If I ran into you in another disguise on the street, I wouldn't recognize you."

"Shall we set up a password, then?"

The boy finally turned to look at me.

"If you say, 'You sure are a beauty,' I'll say, 'Of course. I'm Ms. Gekka.'"

"I just realized your name is fake, too. What, you took it from the flower?" Boy K. smiled wryly. He knows a lot; that's good. "And? Do you have any ideas about those paintings?"

He meant the Danny Bryant pictures he'd brought over the day before. According to the kid, Danny had bought them from a mysterious art dealer, and it was possible that they could help us discover Danny's whereabouts. Today, we were planning to follow that lead to a certain location.

"Yes. Well, to be accurate, I have an idea of someone who may have an idea."

"...That's a pretty roundabout way of putting it. I just assumed we'd be going to the places shown in the pictures."

The paintings he'd brought yesterday had shown certain pastoral landscapes.

"You think Danny Bryant would be there? That's a little too simplistic." As a matter of fact, I had an idea of where the landscapes were as well, but there was something else I wanted to check. "Let's go see the artist behind those paintings."

That had been our ultimate goal.

"The thing is, we aren't quite *ready*. Shall we wander around town until then? I just moved here, you see," I said, beginning to walk away.

"So you want me to show you around? Unfortunately, there isn't much to this place. The town's not that interesting." With a small sigh, he came up beside me and began to walk me through this working-class neighborhood, a stone's throw away from the big city.

"I recommend that pain de mie shop. They'll be all sold out by now, though." The boy pointed at a bakery across the street. There was a big, eye-catching sign with the shop name on it: La Rollebarca. ...Instead of "barcarolle"?

"That's a great name, if I do say so myself."

"Why are you talking up the name of the bakery?"

I wish he wouldn't just hand out that sort of information so easily.

"A while back, a robber forced his way into that place. Stuff happened, I resolved the incident, and they gave me the right to name their bakery," Boy K. explained.

"You said there's nothing to say about this town, and then you have a story like that? That's impressive." *Also, I want the details on the stuff that happened.*

"Oh, and that penny-candy store over there."

Rudely ignoring my comeback, the boy pointed out an old-time candy store. At the back of the shop, in a small, raised area floored with tatami mats, the elderly lady who ran it was drinking tea.

"That old hag..."

"You're suddenly being awfully rude."

"Even if you get a winning wrapper, she says her vision's all blurry and she can't read it, so she won't let you trade it in for your prize."

"Oh, she is rotten and a hag."

I felt sharp eyes zero in on us from within the shop, and the boy and I set off like a pair of racewalkers. *This is a fun town.*

"Oh, right. Gekka. Want to talk to your future self?"

"No, no, this is an everyday small talk conversation; don't start introducing a plot hook."

Nah, I wanted him to keep going. This was getting more and more entertaining. The kid's daily routine might have been more adventurous than mine.

"There's this rumor that if you use the phone booth under that pedestrian bridge, you can talk with yourself from five minutes in the future."

"If that's true, then I'd like to ask if that future me is still getting along with a boy by the name of Kimihiko Kimizuka."

"I interest you that much?"

"As a subject of observation, yes."

While we were having that delightful conversation...

"Dine and dash! Catch him!" a man roared behind us. We turned around, and—

"Oww..."

Boy K. groaned. The young man who'd come running up behind us had shoved him out of the way.

"You really do have it rough, don't you?"

Even as I sympathized with the kid on the pavement, I turned my back to him and went after the fleeing diner. A few seconds later, I'd caught him.

"...Great. All according to plan." Still sitting on his butt on the sidewalk, Boy K. flashed me a thumbs-up.

"You know, we just might make a good team." He'd attract the incidents, and I'd resolve them in the blink of an eye.

If we did that, though, I suspected he'd find twice as much trouble.

After Boy K. and I had strolled around town a little more, I got a text. The sender was one of those people who were vital to my work: a Man in Black. I'd had them investigating *all sorts of backroom business deals* that had been conducted in this town over the past three years. These were the various incidents Fuubi had told me about on the phone earlier: drug deals, political bribes, reselling goods to evade taxes, etc. Danny Bryant had mentioned buying paintings from a certain female art dealer; he clearly hadn't bought them through regular channels, and I'd focused on that.

I'd asked the Men in Black to research underground sales routes for me. Although they held one of the twelve Tuner positions, they were also an organization with countless members around the world. They acted as our hands and feet, our eyes and ears, and took on missions for which they received no fame or credit.

"This is the place. *She's* in here."

Boy K. and I were outside the art gallery the Man in Black had just told me about. It was close to the penny-candy store we had seen earlier, on the second floor of a building in a web of back alleys. Still, it was the sort of place you wouldn't just stumble onto.

According to Boy K., Danny Bryant had said something about buying the paintings from a female art dealer he'd just happened to run into in town, but I'd started to doubt that statement.

"Why here, though?"

Boy K. didn't have a handle on the situation yet, and before we walked into the gallery, he was watching me dubiously.

"I'm told the owner of this place is suspected of tax evasion. I thought there were similarities with the art dealer who sold Danny Bryant those paintings illegally." I explained my theory but kept quiet about the Men in Black.

Needless to say, Fuubi also had this information. However, as a cop, she couldn't act unless she had clear evidence. I was here to conduct an illegal raid.

"So the Fiend with Twenty Faces can transform into a tax official now? ...Well, it does sound like it's worth checking."

I could if I wanted to. Although I'd asked the Men in Black to handle it this time.

"I'll tell you the details once we're inside."

We exchanged looks, then opened the door to the art gallery.

Bright lights illuminated the room, and the gallery's white walls were covered with framed pictures.

"Oh, welcome."

A pale woman stepped out of a room in the back and saw us. She seemed to be in her early thirties; her smile was beautiful, but friendly. "I'm afraid I was planning to close in a few minutes," she said. She was the gallery's owner, Krone, and most likely the one who sold those paintings to Danny.

"You were? I'm glad we made it; I wanted to visit this place today, no matter what," I said, playing innocent. I'd assumed the conversation would go more smoothly if we visited when no one was there, so I'd killed quite a bit of time with Boy K. And it seems we'd timed it just right: We were the only ones in the gallery. Once I'd made sure of that, I got down to business. "I wanted to discuss the *counterfeits* you sell here."

Krone's gentle smile vanished. She walked briskly to the entrance, hung up the CLOSED sign, and came back.

"If you're going to be that obvious, I won't have any questions left to ask."

Of course, I'd already felt certain when I first decided to come here.

"...Who are you? Not the police, surely." Grim-faced, Krone surveyed me from the tips of my toes to the top of my head.

Not at the moment, anyway.

"You sold counterfeits to a relative of ours. Your gallery handles these, doesn't it?"

I showed her photos I'd saved on my phone of the oil paintings Danny Bryant had collected.

"...I know nothing about those."

She certainly didn't look like she knew nothing, but we'd ignore that for now.

"So Danny really did end up buying fakes?" Boy K. shrugged in apparent disappointment. "Well, I doubt he'd regret it anyway." He gave a weak smile. "But how did you know the paintings were counterfeits, Gekka? You're not really…"

It's true that while I was passing myself off as the owner of an antique shop, I couldn't actually tell fake antiques and pieces of fine art from real ones. Even so…

"It's simple. If those paintings were real, no ordinary person would have been able to afford them."

All the pictures Danny Bryant had would have cost upward of fifty million yen each, *if they'd been real*. I couldn't appraise the paintings themselves, but I knew roughly how much fine art would cost.

"…I see. There's no way he could have just picked these up, then. He's always short on money." Boy K. nodded, smirking. "Are all the paintings here like that?"

He didn't seem to know much about art; he scanned the gallery, maybe wondering whether the paintings on the walls were fake as well.

"No, probably not."

I was hardly an expert myself, so it was hard to say for sure. Still, I had memorized information on paintings above a certain price level, in conjunction with their artist profiles, and not one of the paintings here was a match in that database. All of these had to be originals, drawn by artists who weren't widely known yet. There was no point in counterfeiting works of art that weren't famous.

"Still, they're pretty expensive." The boy frowned, reading the price tags below the paintings. I knew how he felt, but the boy could be quite tactless.

"Well, quality is expensive." Krone finally broke her uncomfortable silence. She could probably tell that we weren't going anywhere until she talked to us.

"Of course, that isn't to say they'll sell," she murmured with a self-deprecating smile. If there was a reason to sell these paintings at high prices when their artists weren't famous, it was…

"You're not doing this for the money, are you?" I asked.

Krone flinched, freezing up.

She'd said so herself, just a moment ago: quality is expensive. In other words, what she was after was...

"You're not selling, you're buying. As far as you're concerned, that's your job. Isn't that right?"

There was a brief silence.

"In the end, art is business, you see." Krone sighed; she looked almost resigned. "It has nothing to do with how well the picture was painted. Fine art is a business, and the *self-proclaimed experts* deliberately create new stars on a daily basis. Someone decides that *a particular painting will be considered outstanding.* There's nothing genuine there."

I see. It sounded similar to how the fashion world worked. It wasn't that what was selling became popular; it was made popular so that it would sell. Someone decided that a certain thing would be "in" this year, and that was all it took.

Krone was asking the world if it was really okay with that.

"I don't buy artists' names. I buy their skill. I want to pursue 'the real thing' in art as well."

As she spoke, she gazed at the paintings by unknown artists that hung in the gallery. The experts hadn't discovered these artists yet, so their pictures didn't stand out on the market. Even so, there was solid talent behind them, and Krone purchased them at high prices.

"If that's your ambition, then why did you sell counterfeits?" Boy K. asked, pointing out the apparent contradiction in her behavior.

"That's also an outgrowth of my ideals," Krone told him. "The paintings you showed me really were replicas. I've been in this business for more than ten years, but even I couldn't tell at first. I knew, logically, that those paintings shouldn't be in Japan. That was how I managed to identify them as counterfeits; it wasn't the result of a formal appraisal."

She'd identified them the same way I had. However, unlike me, her knowledge of fine art was deep and detailed, and even she hadn't immediately been able to identify those paintings as fakes. That was how polished the copies were.

"I set a price not on the paintings themselves, but on the skills of the painter who'd made such perfect imitations."

"Wait, did Danny buy them from you for the same reason?"

"No. As a matter of fact, he asked me to do this." At last, Krone gave us the information we wanted. "He said he knew an artist with extraordinary skills. He'd never seen anything like it before. He asked if I could visit them and buy their artwork."

It seems Danny's story about coincidentally running into Krone and buying those pictures really had been a lie. Had the two of them been business acquaintances all along? Then why had he kept quiet about it? He hadn't even told the kid...

"If he wanted the pictures that badly, why not just go get them himself? Why was he so roundabout?" The idea seemed to mystify the boy.

"I couldn't say. I only knew him through our business deals, and he never let others know what he was really thinking." Krone gazed at the one blank space on the white wall. "I think he must have had some lofty goal. ...That said—and you may be angry with me for saying this—his eyes seemed to be focused on something in the distance, and it frightened me a little."

Danny Bryant had always had several faces.

A former Federation Government spy, and a traitor to the group.

A private detective, and an enigmatic wandering handyman.

A surrogate dad for Boy K., whom he'd taken from the children's home.

Which one was real, and what had he been trying to accomplish? If I met him, would I have figured it out?

"Still, who would have thought he had someone like you?" Krone turned back, gazing at Boy K. Then she gave a sudden smile. "Now, what's next? Have you finished your business here? It's true that I sold illegal counterfeits, so if you plan to turn me in, I'll have no choice but to comply." Jokingly, Krone held out her hands as if she were waiting to be cuffed.

"No, that isn't my job. More importantly, there was one last thing I wanted to know." I asked her my most pressing question. "Where can we find the person who painted those counterfeits?"

After leaving the gallery, Boy K. and I headed straight for the train station.

We were bound for the Hokuriku region. Apparently, that was where the artist lived. Krone had given us their address, and now we were a little closer to our goal.

Why had Danny Bryant cared so much about an artist who copied paintings? Why had he entrusted those pictures to Boy K. and disappeared? In search of the answers to those questions, Boy K. and I boarded the last bullet train of the day and headed for the Hokuriku region.

When we reached our destination, it was near midnight, and we decided to spend the night at a business hotel that was directly connected to the station. Postponing our visit to the artist until the next morning, we checked in right away and took our luggage to our room.

"Mm, a freshly washed pillow and coverlet. Paradise." I flopped face down onto the fluffy mattress. Just getting to sleep on a soft bed was a luxury. Once I begin fighting the world's enemies in earnest, I doubted I'd get to indulge in these luxuries, and so I made up my mind to savor this everyday happiness while I could.

"Come on, you, too. Aren't you going to bounce on the bed?"

"What am I, a kid?"

"Yes. *You* are."

The boy pouted back at me. It was pretty cute.

He sat down on the other bed. "I'm used to spending the night away from home, and it's not the first time I've been to this area. There's really nothing to be so excited about," he said bluntly.

"Huh. When were you here before? On a school trip? Did you manage to enjoy it, even though you ended up by yourself?"

"I was here a year ago, it wasn't a school trip, and don't make random guesses and start feeling sorry for me over them."

"Lucky you. This time you got to come here with a gorgeous older woman."

"Except your personality sucks, so I basically break even."

"Ah, so even with a flawed personality, I'm so beautiful that it balances out."

"Quit with the optimism gymnastics. Your face is pretty much special effects makeup anyway, right?" The boy looked at me closely.

What a shame I can't show him my real face. Should I let him see it at one point and call it one of my disguises, and watch how he reacts?

"And hey, how come we're sharing a room?" It seemed a bit late to complain about that, but he averted his eyes.

"Because we have to; they only had one vacancy. Oh, is this due to that odd predisposition of yours, too? What if you're actually the one who caused this sleepover?"

"I didn't cause it, I just got dragged into it. By you." This time, the boy looked me in the eye as he spoke.

"Well, should we play cards all night?"

"No. I'm going to sleep."

"In mysteries, that means you're the next to die. It's all right, though: The detective will protect you."

"You're going to act as a detective now? You're one strange 'fiend.'" The boy looked exasperated, but he was definitely smiling.

The first time I saw him, he'd appeared to have given up on everything. Back then, somehow, his profile had struck me as beautiful. When I saw him smile, though, I liked it even more. ...For no particular reason.

"It was cold out there; I'd like to soak in the bath and warm up. Want to come in with me?"

"......No. There's no reason to do that."

"What about saving water?"

"We don't need to worry about saving water at a hotel."

"When you turned me down a second ago, you hesitated a bit."

"If you're gonna pretend to let it go, don't bring it up later!" The boy sighed, shoulders slumping.

But then...

"Can we be serious for a minute?" He lifted his head, gazing at me.

Apparently, playtime was over for the moment. I motioned for him to go on.

"Gekka—who are you?" Boy K. was moving toward the truth of the Fiend with Twenty Faces. "That guy, Danny... He never told me anything. Not what he was thinking, or what job he was working on, or who he really was."

"So you're asking me instead?"

"I know it's kinda weird," the boy admitted. "But... Somehow, you two seem sort of similar to me."

I hadn't been expecting that.

I'd never met Danny Bryant. I knew he'd been employed by the Federation Government before, that he was a handyman and Boy K.'s father figure, and a treacherous spy—but these titles were all I knew about him. What about Danny had reminded Boy K. of me?

"Then what is it that you want to know about me?"

I couldn't reveal that I was the Ace Detective without violating Federation

Government rules. Even so, if I didn't tell him anything important, I might lose his trust. That was why I decided to give him a tiny peek behind the curtain.

Boy K. immediately started asking question after question. "Why are you looking for information on Danny? Is it because you want to, or are you following orders from somebody else?"

I see. So that had been on his mind. Since we'd been after the same things until now, he hadn't pushed for details about it. If we were going to stay together for a while, though, he'd probably decided we needed to be on the same page.

"At first, you said Danny was suspected of a theft. That's a fairly petty crime, though; you're going to great lengths just to catch a thief."

The boy's sharp eyes focused on me.

I'd known I wouldn't be able to put him off forever. Considering what I'd been doing lately, it was no wonder he'd become suspicious and doubtful. In a move to regain his trust, I began to tell him about my job, sticking to things that wouldn't get me in trouble.

"I have only one answer to both of your questions: I'm investigating Danny Bryant because I was ordered to."

"So you don't have any personal business with him?"

I shook my head.

To be honest, I was curious about the whole situation. The fact that Ice Doll seemed almost too concerned about Danny was strange, and the way Boy K. was trying to hide something about him tugged at me as well. However, those concerns were secondary; my orders were to come first.

"Who ordered you?"

"I can't tell you that. Even if I did, I doubt you'd be able to understand right now. It's an adults-only sort of thing," I said, and the boy rolled his eyes. And then…

"In that case, as far as Danny and I are concerned, are they an enemy? Or are they on our side?"

Oh. That, huh? I thought. Boy K. must have wanted to know about this the most.

He must be extra sensitive to crises that threatened Danny Bryant. Either that, or he'd picked up on the presence of an enemy and was trying to figure out who they were. The only thing I could say now, and do for him, was...

"I promise you one thing." The boy turned back to face me. "As long as I'm standing between you and them, I won't let them be outright hostile toward you. I'll work to guarantee that both sides benefit as much as possible."

"...So you're a negotiator?"

"My job title doesn't matter." One thing was certain, though. "As long as you assist me, I'll reward you. If you ask me for help, I'll always respond. And then for the first time, we'll be equals." I held out my hand. The boy gave it a long, steady look. Then, as if he'd made up his mind, he grasped it and squeezed back.

"I get the feeling there's too much emphasis on protecting me, though."

"Well, I'm older, so there is a bit of that."

We'd just reached a formal agreement.

"All right, I'm going to go take that bath. What about you, kid?"

"Morning's going to come early, so I'm hitting the sack."

Wow, he's not cute at all.

◇ May 2   Kimihiko Kimizuka

Just after midnight, I was lying on the hotel bed, half asleep, when the phone by my pillow alerted me to a call.

The caller was—Danny Bryant.

With a small gasp, I went over to the window, then tapped the TALK button.

"Hey there. You're *over here*, aren't you?" The voice from the receiver sounded more appalled than angry. As I hesitated, not sure how to answer, I heard a heavy sigh. "There's nobody nearby, right? You're alone?"

I looked around to make sure. "Yeah. I've been alone since I was born, including now."

"Ha-ha. Good answer. I give it sixty points." Danny laughed. He's a pretty tough grader. "—So? Why did you come out here, too?" His voice suddenly dipped. He was slightly angry after all. "I'm pretty sure I told you to watch the fort."

I remembered what Danny had said three nights ago, that he was headed out to do a hairy job, so he wouldn't be home for a while.

I'd spent the next day as usual, just as he'd told me...but then I'd reconsidered and tried to follow him as best I could.

"Geez, brat. Do as you're told, wouldja?" Well, I hadn't. On the other end of the line, I could tell Danny was stumped.

"I'm here by coincidence. I got this intense craving for some Toyama black ramen."

"Sure. Well, there's a ton of instant ramen in the cupboard. Go right back home and boil some water. I recommend letting it sit for two and a half minutes; the noodles are nice and chewy then."

Okay. So he wasn't going to truly respond until I was honest with him. "You were the one who said I'd have to be a con man who could fool cops and detectives."

I thought I heard a little gasp on the other end of the line.

"I'm not the police, kid."

"It's just a metaphor. Whatever you are, it doesn't matter to me. I just..." I couldn't seem to get the words out. "Where are you right now?" I asked instead. I knew he had to be close, but where was he exactly? And also... "What's this hairy job of yours? Does it have something to do with whoever's been after you lately?"

I fired one question after another at Danny.

He stayed silent, and then... "Why are you asking me all that now?" His voice was perfectly calm. "We've never had a serious conversation before. We've never meddled in each other's business. Those were the rules. Why would you break them?" He wanted to know what was behind my change of heart, but he'd just said it himself.

"You're always wandering off, and I never know what you're doing. Even when you went somewhere for a job, you didn't go out of your way to tell me. And yet this time, you said the job was going to be tricky...and you also said you wouldn't be back for a while. Why?"

Maybe it was just a hunch, something I couldn't trust. Back then, though, Danny had sounded like he was steeling himself for something. "I'm going to ask you one more time, Danny Bryant. Where are you? I'll meet up with you right away," I added.

"What can you do?"

"I dunno. Maybe nothing."

"Then why would you come here?" Danny sighed, sounding irritated.

I gave it a little thought. "You're the reason I'm like this, and I want to know what's happening to you." I also wanted to see it through to the end. That was all.

After half a minute of silence...

"...We'll meet up in twenty hours. I'll contact you with the location later," Danny said. I'd worn him down. "You're even more of a pain now than you were when I first met you." He seemed fondly exasperated now.

"Is it okay if I take that as a compliment?"

"Go study Japanese, read some books, and underline all the characters' feelings."

"What do I do when the narrator's unreliable? The protagonist might be a con man."

"Ha-ha. You'll just have to read between the lines. Brush up your communication skills and work on reading emotions."

Hm. After so many years living alone, this could be the highest hurdle I'd faced yet.

"If you can't do that, then gather evidence."

"Evidence? You're telling me to look beyond what they're saying?"

"Right. If you don't know what a guy is thinking, start by observing. Look, listen, talk, and collect information. He'll probably lie sometimes; people do that. So don't go taking everything at face value. Weigh objective testimony, evidence, and facts."

Danny's words gradually grew more intense.

"Analysis, theory, and thought: Those are always important. Think of what that person has done. Think about what it really means. Don't get stuck on words; don't be fooled. If you don't understand the human heart, then trust what you see. What you should believe is reality. Learn about people that way," he finished.

"If I do, will I understand them someday?" I was sure I still didn't understand half of what Danny just said. I asked anyway, in case.

"Yeah, I think you will," Danny said, showing a strong amount of confidence in his theory. "But. If you ever find yourself in a situation you really can't handle, I bet you'll run into somebody who'll give you a better answer."

"What, so you're just passing the buck in the end? Again?" I broke into a joyless smile.

"Ha-ha. Well, don't stress out about it. For now, just tuck the idea away in a corner of your mind." His tone grew uncharacteristically soft. "Don't worry. Whenever you're driven by necessity, you'll meet the people you need to meet. That's true now and forever."

It almost sounded as if Danny was trying to give my problematic predisposition new meaning. "I'll call you again," he said, and hung up.

◆ May 2   Siesta

Early the next morning, we left the hotel and headed for the place where Krone had told us the artist lived.

It took us a bit over two hours after transferring between trains and buses. The place was located well outside the city, and as we made our way toward it on foot, a white building that looked like a church came into view on the other side of the grassy plain.

"It's a children's home," Boy K. muttered behind me. "I can hear kids' voices. It doesn't seem like a regular school, though."

I'd heard that he'd lived at a facility before Danny Bryant took him in. That was why he had jumped straight to that possibility. We had that in common; I'd once lived in a facility with other kids my age, too. During my days there, I'd—

"Gekka, what's wrong?"

The next thing I knew, the boy had come up beside me and was staring at my face, seeming puzzled. "Do you feel sick? Did you eat too much?"

Somehow, he'd picked up on the fact that I wasn't feeling well. He was worried, but I wasn't happy that he immediately jumped to overeating.

"I don't believe my disguise is so flimsy that you could pick up on changes in my complexion."

"You slowed down a bit. I thought maybe you'd eaten too much, and it was weighing you down. Or maybe..." the boy said, walking slowly beside me. "Is there a reason you don't want to reach that building?"

I didn't think there was. ...But could I be forgetting something?

Was I frightened of this shelter for children? —Why would I be?

"Let's go."

I didn't know. Which was why there was nothing for it but to press forward.

I'd solve the mysteries in my life by myself.

"That has to be why I became a detective," I murmured, too softly for anyone else to hear.

When we reached the white building, there was a man in a wheelchair out in the front yard, watering the flowers. I called out to him. "Excuse me. Can we have a moment?"

The man slowly turned around, wheelchair and all.

His features seemed European, and he might have been in his seventies. He had a dignified appearance, and his white hair had been carefully styled. The combination made him seem very refined. I could easily imagine him getting up out of that chair at any moment and drawing himself up to his full height, even if I knew he couldn't now.

"We're—"

"I thought you might come someday."

Boy K. and I exchanged looks. The kid shook his head; he didn't know this man, either.

Even so, the two of us gave our names, and the old man introduced himself as Jekyll. "Well, come in," he said with a gentle smile. He turned and propelled his chair toward the front entrance, which was flush with the ground. He seemed to know why we were there.

"You think it's a trap?" the boy whispered to me.

"I'd say the odds are fifty-fifty."

"Great. Okay, what do we do?"

"There's a fifty percent chance that we'll get results and come out of this unscathed, and a fifty percent chance that we'll get injured but still obtain results."

"...So you've already decided we're going."

Exactly. I really like sharp kids.

Jekyll led us down a long corridor to a great hall of some kind. About a dozen children were inside, drawing pictures or putting puzzles together.

"Gekka, look." Boy K. pointed at a spot high on the wall. Watercolors and oil paintings of landscapes and everyday objects hung there. The art styles were all different, but the motley look of the techniques made me think of the person we were searching for.

"Do Grete's paintings interest you fine people?" Jekyll spoke to us politely, even though we were far younger than he was. "Grete" was the name of the artist we were looking for.

"Is she one of the children who live here?"

"She is indeed. Her parents abandoned her, although I won't divulge the specifics. She's been here since she was small."

I could think of a few reasons parents might abandon a child, from their financial circumstances to an unwanted pregnancy. Either way, although Grete's parents should have loved her unconditionally, they'd abandoned her at this facility.

"She has incredible skill, doesn't she?"

The compliment I blurted out was a very common one. As a matter of fact, her pictures were so beautiful that her family and the circumstances she'd been born into just didn't seem important.

"Well, according to Grete, those are originals and still quite unpolished." Smiling a little, the old man gazed up at the landscapes on the wall. "Creating meticulously accurate copies is where her skills really shine. I doubt even the most keen-eyed art dealer could tell her paintings were a fake."

That was exactly what we'd seen happen.

Jekyll continued. "Human faces are constantly changing, so she isn't good at capturing them on canvas. On the other hand, when she uses a static model, she can re-create it perfectly. That's her specialty."

"...At that level, it's basically a superpower," Boy K. said, unsure what to believe. And then...

"Yes, most of these children have similar special abilities or skills. Are you familiar with the word *gifted*? It refers to individuals who are born with advanced intelligence, artistic ability, or creativity."

From his wheelchair, Jekyll gazed at the children who were playing in the large room.

"Here at Sun House, we protect and foster children like that. I have the honor of serving as the facility's representative. ...Although, really, I'm just an old, retired soldier." Jekyll smiled self-deprecatingly.

"You say 'special ability,' but you don't mean things like teleportation or shooting flames from their palms, do you?" I asked.

Jekyll nodded quietly. "That's correct. *It's all within the realm of common sense.* Acquiring and using multiple languages in a short amount of time, or being able to instantly and accurately remember what they've seen... There are also children who excel at reading others' mental states, or who can have lucid dreams voluntarily."

"That seems plenty uncommon to me," Boy K. retorted.

Still smiling, Jekyll elaborated. "No, they're all quite real. The ability to read human emotions can be explained with psychology, and science is working to prove lucid dreams as we speak."

"Then what about Grete?" I asked. How was she able to make counterfeits so perfect that even the experts were fooled?

"She has a rare gift for spatial awareness, and a superior talent for art. Together, they make it possible for her to re-create paintings perfectly. Grete perceives things as detailed schematics," Jekyll explained.

I took another look at the large room, and the children who were in it. Their ages ranged from three to twelve or thirteen. From what we'd just heard, most of them had some sort of special ability, and this facility existed to protect them.

The average person probably would have had a hard time believing that. Even Boy K. was perplexed, with good reason, and he was constantly getting pulled into all sorts of odd things. However, I knew people like the children in this facility... People who were even more gifted, in fact. For example, there was a girl who foresaw events related to global crises. She had once been the prisoner of a certain organization. Did this facility have some other secret as well?

"Would it be possible for us to meet Grete?"

According to Krone, Danny Bryant had discovered the girl's special ability. What was her connection to him? Grete might have information about Danny that we couldn't learn from anyone else. On that thought, I—

"Jekyll! Look at this!" A lively voice interrupted our conversation.

I turned around. A red-haired girl in a white dress was coming toward us, practically dancing. She looked around eleven or twelve. Then she noticed Boy K. and I. "Oh, visitors...?" she said, and slowed down, seeming a little embarrassed.

"You've drawn a new picture?" Jekyll gave her a soft smile.

"Uh-huh! I drew Natalie's portrait today!" Grete cheerfully showed Jekyll a picture of a friend who lived at the facility. It was an original painting of a girl's smiling face. "I wonder if I could draw Danny now, too," Grete murmured a little shyly.

So she really did know him.

"What's your connection to Danny?" Boy K. asked.

For just a moment, Grete froze. Then she realized we were Danny's friends, too. "Um…" she faltered, lifting the canvas so that it hid the lower half of her face. She seemed bashful by nature.

"Danny Bryant is the one who encouraged Grete to polish her art skills," Jekyll explained.

"He worked to protect those like Grete, children with special circumstances. Since getting by in the regular world was going to be difficult for them, he taught them skills that would help them live independently once they left Sun House."

I see: ways to earn money. It all made sense now. Danny must have bought Grete's paintings in order to show her that her ability to create perfect counterfeits could help her earn a living. He'd had Krone, a real art dealer, serve as the middleman so that Grete wouldn't think he was just being kind because he knew her.

"When do you suppose Danny's coming back?" Grete looked down, her expression lonely. "Maybe he's busy with work." From what Ice Doll and Fuubi had said, Danny had disappeared a year ago. Hadn't he visited Sun House since then, either?

"Well, that's a good question." Jekyll looked at us. …Or rather, at Boy K. "He might know."

All our eyes focused on him.

"Do you know what Danny's doing?" Grete asked Boy K. timidly, overcoming her shyness.

"Kid," I said. He shot me a brief glance. "I think it's about time you told me the truth, too, isn't it?"

This was the black box Boy K. had been hiding all this time. I'd been dimly aware that he had some big secret, but I'd been waiting for it to come to the surface.

"You know where Danny Bryant is, don't you?"

I wasn't positive. I'd spent the past few days with him, however, and considering how he'd acted, it was a pretty solid guess.

Jekyll, Grete, and I were all watching him, but Boy K. didn't turn a hair. He just drew one small breath, then filled us in.

"Yeah. Danny's been dead for a year."

◇ May 2   Kimihiko Kimizuka

"Danny, where are you?!" I yelled into the phone when the call finally went through.

It was late at night. Except for me, there was nobody outside.

"...Hey, you sound pretty stressed."

On the other end of the line, Danny sounded like his usual easygoing self, but his breathing seemed a little ragged.

We'd talked before, just after midnight, and had planned to meet up that evening. I waited and waited, but Danny never showed up. I'd called his phone again and again, and this was the first time he'd picked up.

"—! What are you doing?! Why didn't you come?!"

"Ha-ha. I warned you. You can't let con men fool you, Detective."

Who's a detective?! I wanted to shout back at him. My fingers tightened around my phone.

Every so often, I heard something that sounded like a groan. Was he hurt? "I'll be right there. Danny, where are you?" Even as I asked, I was racing toward the spot on the coast where we'd planned to meet earlier. The black ocean spread out in front of me, unchanging and endless.

"...There's one thing I need to tell you."

"The only thing you need to tell me is where you are right now!"

"There's bound to come a day when you wonder why life refuses to go your way, why it's so cruel. You'll lose hope." Danny didn't answer my question. He seemed to be speaking from experience. "It won't matter how happy you were up till then. Maybe you had the best horoscope in the paper that day; maybe you were just picking out a cake for a beloved member of your family. None of that will matter. The devil of misfortune never gives a shit about how it's supposed to go."

"...I didn't know you'd been married."

"Ha-ha. You never asked."

It's not like you would have told me if I had.

"—! When despair comes on the heels of tepid happiness, it hurts like hell."

Danny's voice was trembling, but not from emotion. There was something physically wrong with him. Even so, he kept talking.

"You'll think, 'I didn't know life could get so ugly.' You won't feel anything as simple as anger or sadness. All you'll feel is…futility. Emptiness with nowhere to go."

I'd been running without a break, and my chest was starting to hurt. My legs were still moving, and I could still swing my arms, but my heart and lungs couldn't keep up, and each breath was a choking gasp.

"Humans are funny, though. When night falls, we get sleepy, and then we wake up in the morning with our stomachs growling. We think, 'So, what, was that despair even real? Was I just faking? Huh. My body's still trying to live.' It'll make you think survival instincts are a royal pain in the butt. Even so," Danny went on. "That's what humans are. No matter how reality refuses to go your way, you've gotta keep on living."

His rant might have been directed at himself or at the world, but in the next moment, his usual dauntless optimism was back.

"Even if you've lost one way of life, you can choose a new one. We have to. That's how we keep living. You get it, don'cha?"

He sounded as if he were lecturing a kid.

"…No, I don't. I don't get it." I was out of breath. My feet caught on the sand, and I finally collapsed.

"Ha-ha. Well, you don't have to understand right away. Remember what I told you earlier, though. Someday, you'll—"

Just then, I heard other voices on his end of the line. One woman, and a man who wasn't Danny. Who was it? Who was there with him?

"…Sorry. Time's up, I guess."

"What are you talking about?! Danny!"

"Listen up, Kimihiko." For the first time I could remember, Danny said my name. And then…

"You…live on."

Live on.

Right after that, a gunshot rang out.

That was the last time I heard Danny's real voice. Three days before my birthday.

◆ May 2   Siesta

"And that's how I lost Danny last year."

That was the secret Boy K. had kept hidden all this time—a full year, to the day.

What had happened to him then—or rather, to Danny Bryant?

The truth behind Danny's disappearance was the worst one possible: He was already dead.

"He won't be coming back here. He's gone."

When Jekyll heard that, he silently closed his eyes. Grete looked stunned, unable to process what she'd just learned. I was the only one who managed to speak.

"Who did it?"

According to the kid, Danny had spoken as if he knew he'd reached the end of his life, and he'd heard other voices and a gunshot. It was only natural to assume that someone had shot and killed Danny.

"I have no clue. ...Some of the jobs he did would have made him enemies. It's highly likely that one of them decided to settle their score with him."

It made sense. He was a former Federation Government spy; had someone been after him because of that? Maybe he'd been on an undercover mission, and his cover had gotten blown, so they'd executed him. Or it might have been some anti-government group who'd wanted to pry classified information out of him—

"So that's why you kept asking whether I was Danny Bryant's enemy."

Danny was already dead. Boy K. had no idea who'd killed him. Since I was still pursuing him, he'd been trying to gather information while pretending to help me.

Thinking back, I realized that the boy's attitude toward me had clearly warmed the moment I brought Danny up at the police station. He might already have been weighing the possibility that I was *worth using*.

In other words, our interests had lined up. We'd been using each other: Me in an attempt to find Danny Bryant, and Boy K. in an attempt to uncover the truth behind his death.

"In that case, I really wish you'd told me the truth a bit sooner."

We'd acted as if we were cooperating for the sake of our own goals, but I'd suspected Boy K. was hiding something. I never would have guessed it was Danny Bryant's death, though.

"Yeah, I feel bad about that. Still..." Boy K. gave a crooked smile. "Danny told me to be a con man so that I could fool cops and detectives."

Goosebumps ran across my skin.

Cops and detectives—he had to have picked those words by coincidence. Even so, it felt as if he'd figured out what I really was, and I felt a weird sinking sensation in the pit of my stomach.

But there was no way the kid could have unmasked me so easily.

...Actually, in this case, he wouldn't have been the one who'd seen through me, would he?

"No, not possible."

A certain theory crossed my mind, and I shook my head, hastily getting rid of it.

There was one more thing that kept tugging at me, though.

"Kid? Is Danny Bryant really...?" I didn't say *dead*. I didn't have to.

"...Good question. I dunno." The boy didn't deny the possibility he was wrong. He hadn't actually seen Danny's body after all. He only had indirect evidence.

"I was hoping you might turn something up, Gekka. I thought Danny was dead, and here was this mysterious police officer who was looking for him... And then you were actually the Fiend with Twenty Faces, acting on orders from some organization. I thought you might know a few secrets."

But as it turned out, I hadn't known the truth about Danny's death. Maybe the boy was disappointed in me.

"If you're confessing this now, though..."

"Yeah. I thought if I showed my cards, new information might turn up."

As a matter of fact, by coming here, we'd learned that Danny had been involved with Sun House, a facility that sheltered children with special circumstances. Some of his secrets must still be hidden, and they were probably linked to the truth behind his death. That meant we still had to—

"That can't be true!" the girl with us shrieked.

Grete shook her head again and again, denying what we'd said. "I mean, he promised! Danny... Danny's not—!" She wiped her tears away. Then she turned her back to us and ran.

The children who'd been playing in the big room all looked over, startled.

"Nice. You made a girl cry." I sighed.

"It's that guy's fault for vanishing on everybody," Boy K. said.

Still, I'd seen his expression as he murmured those words, and I really couldn't scold him.

"May I ask you to...?" Jekyll gave us an awkward smile. The kid and I exchanged looks, then went after Grete.

Not even five minutes later, we spotted the girl's small back. She was outside, on a cape with a view of the ocean, watching the waves roll in.

"Grete," I called out to her.

Her shoulders flinched. Then she sniffled. "I can't draw Danny's face."

She was talking about her pictures. Grete always drew by making perfect copies of subjects. However...

"Because you're bad with expressions and other moving things?"

The old man had told us that was why she only made copies of existing drawings.

"Jekyll always glosses it over like that, but that's not actually why. *I can't see people's faces.*"

Face blindness. The condition came to mind right away.

It was a type of neurological disorder: the inability to recognize human faces. A sufferer could perceive eyes, noses, and other features separately, but they couldn't see them as a single integrated "face."

This meant that people with face blindness couldn't pick up on changes in human expressions, and they were unable to tell others apart, even if they were close friends. That was why Grete—

"And so you always drew things that didn't change."

"Funny, huh?" the girl said, laughing at herself. "All I can do is see people's eyes, noses, and mouths as symbols and paint them that way. If that's enough, I can sort of paint people; it's just like making a copy. But..." She turned around. Her large eyes were filled with tears. "When I finish a picture like that, *I can't tell if it's really finished.* I still don't know what the face of the person I love looks like."

At this point, we hardly needed to ask who that person was.

"I promised. I said I'd beat this thing someday, and I'd paint Danny's portrait. Then I'd show it to him and have him tell me whether it really looked like him, *whether I'd gotten it right or not.*"

That was the promise Grete had made with Danny. Now that dream would never come true. What she'd heard from Boy K. had dashed her hopes.

"Still, somewhere in my heart, I think I knew. This whole year, I waited and waited. I did think Danny might never come back. But..." Grete wiped her tears away with her palms, again and again, and managed to say the rest of her sentence. "I wanted him to be safe and happy somewhere...!"

Even if their promise never came true—as long as Danny had been alive somewhere, that would have been enough.

I was an outsider, and I had no idea how close the two of them had been. It would have been presumptuous of me to assume that they must have been like father and daughter. The tale they'd woven was theirs alone.

And so I couldn't take that step forward. I couldn't reach out and wipe Grete's tears away. It probably wasn't my job, or a job for any detective. You can't use egocentric kindness and thoughtfulness to save people. In that case, I'd keep doing things my way and—

"I don't know Danny's face, either."

The kid lacked the kindness and thoughtfulness I had—but he went up to Grete without hesitating and spoke to her before I could. "He never genuinely laughed around me; he didn't cry, and he didn't get mad. That guy never showed me who he really was."

Right: This wasn't kindness or thoughtfulness. It was objective fact, based in two years' worth of Boy K.'s experiences.

Speaking gently, he offered Grete what sympathy he could. "So I don't know what he looks like, either. I still remember lots of things about him, though. His voice was hoarse from liquor and cigarettes, and his hair pomade had this really cloying smell. Oh yeah, and he was always going up and patting people's shoulders. His hands were really rough. I'm sure I never knew his true self, but even after a year, I remember his voice and that smell and the way his hands felt. You do, too, don't you?"

"...Uh-huh. I do, too." On the other side of the boy, Grete smiled just a little, although her eyes were red.

"Besides, when Danny looked at your paintings, he seemed happy. He said he wanted to treasure those beautiful pictures of yours more than any sound argument or his own philosophy."

When Grete heard that, her eyes widened, and she teared up again. "...I see. I know it's late to do it now, but I do want to draw his portrait."

The wind blew, softly ruffling her red hair.

"Yeah. I'm sure he's waiting for that, too," the boy said, encouraging her gently.

From where I stood, I couldn't see his face.

"—I'm tired."

I'd taken off my mask, and as I was gazing at my face in the hotel washroom's mirror, the words slipped out.

This was my own face, no makeup. Pale skin and blue eyes. My face might seem grown-up compared to other kids my age, but objectively speaking, my youth was obvious.

With a small sigh, I stripped off my clothes, then left the washroom. There was no one else in the room.

Boy K. and I had parted ways at the children's home. He'd had something he wanted to think about on his own, and when Jekyll had generously offered to let him stay the night, he'd accepted.

Meanwhile, I'd ridden buses and trains back the way we'd come, returning to our hotel. I had several jobs to do.

"It's been a while since I was alone."

I toppled over onto the bed in my underwear.

Now that no one was here to see, it should be okay to be this sloppy. Curling up within the sheets when I was practically naked was oddly soothing. Was this what being in the womb felt like?

"I'd better call in."

I couldn't just laze around. I had new information about Danny Bryant, and that meant I had a report to make. I picked up my phone and considered calling Ice Doll, the Federation Government official. First, I'd tell her that Danny had been sheltering children with special abilities.

"I wonder if she knew."

I got the feeling that Danny's involvement with the kids hadn't been connected to the spy work he'd done for the Federation Government.

In that case, had it been a personal job? It was also likely that job had somehow gotten Danny killed. That much was clear from the fact that it had happened while he was working nearby.

In that case, had the enemy—the killer—been trying to keep Danny from helping those kids? But why?

"Maybe it's still a little too early to report this to the higher-ups."

I went over what I needed to do. First, I wanted to figure out who Danny had been up against last year. In order to do that, I'd probably have to leave the area.

There was one more thing I wanted to think about carefully before I contacted Ice Doll: Danny Bryant's death itself.

Of course, the possibility of his death had crossed my mind. It was the first explanation that should have occurred to me, really.

Even so, because of Boy K., I'd begun to eliminate that possibility. He and Danny had been practically family, and although he'd known the truth, he hadn't let anything slip.

It had seemed as if he'd completely forgotten about Danny's death and was working with me to find out the truth. The reality was different: He'd known that Danny was dead and used me in an attempt to learn more about it.

"*Clever* isn't quite the word."

When I'd first met Boy K., and when I'd learned that he was pretending to be the culprit behind that murder incident, I'd thought he was a very crafty kid. He wasn't afraid to sacrifice himself in order to reach his goals, and he was able to carry out meticulous plans.

That might not have been the case, though. He could feel genuine fear. He was scared of losing something. And yet *he was able to hide it completely.*

At first, I'd thought he was a perfectly ordinary boy, then I'd learned he was very clever, and now he frightened me a little.

I'd thought we were alike. Neither of us was temperamental, and we kept a similar distance between ourselves and others. ...But he wasn't like me.

He did have strong emotions, impulses, and wishes, but for the sake of his goal, he could stifle them all. He could pretend to be a delightful, engaging person. The mask of the Fiend with Twenty Faces had nothing on his.

"Which face is your real one?"

I stretched my hand out toward the ceiling. This hand wasn't capable of stripping off his mask yet, most likely.

"...What am I thinking?" Suddenly, I realized I was planning to keep him in my life. Was it for the sake of the mission? Or was it—

"I guess I really am tired."

I let my hand fall to my forehead.

Desperately, I banished that second possibility from my mind.

"Will you sacrifice your companions again?"

The voice of the great evil echoed in my head.

I know.

I know, so get out of here. I brushed the illusion away with my right hand.

"—Oh, you finally picked up."

Just then, a girl's voice spoke from the smartphone by my pillow.

Apparently, a call had come in, and I'd unintentionally hit the TALK button. ...In video call mode, too.

"Oh, Mia. It's been a while, huh." Collecting myself, I responded. I'd said "It's been a while" on instinct, but it had only been a week or so since the last time we'd talked. I'd met Mia Whitlock in London, right before I left for Japan.

"Yes, it's been a week... Wha— B-Boss? What are you wearing?"

I was lazing around on the bed, holding the phone up high, when Mia started panicking. Oh, right, I was still in my underwear.

"You're a guardian of the world. Get it together, would you?"

Mia blushed, partially covering her face with her hands, peeking through her fingers. *What is she trying to do?*

"Sorry, sorry. You caught me in the middle of changing." Telling a small white lie, I set down my phone and put on a nearby bathrobe. "And? What did you need?"

Mia was the Oracle, a Tuner like me. Since we traded information about Seed on a regular basis, we often talked like this, but today hadn't been one of our scheduled meetings.

"Well, I may have finally found something that could change the future recorded in the sacred text." Mia's voice sounded serious.

The sacred text was a book of prophecies about global crises, written by a series of Oracles. At present, it foretold my defeat at the hands of one of Seed's executives. We'd been spending our days working out a strategy that would change that future.

"A possibility? Don't tell me—is this about the Singularity?" I asked, picking up my phone again. The Singularity was the one thing that could change the future as it was written. Mia had once explained that the future branched out in many directions, with that individual as the point of origin.

However, knowing when and where the Singularity would be born was nearly impossible. Even the Oracle had to wait until she *just happened* to spot them. ...But I'd definitely heard Mia say she might have found a way to change the future.

My heart was pounding, whether I wanted it to or not.

And then Mia told me the identity of the Singularity she'd seen.

"...Boss?"

After a short silence, she called out to me, worried.

"No, it's all right. It's just..."

I really have been hearing that name an awful lot lately, I thought.

A certain girl's tale 3

"And that's where the story links up. I see."
I closed the journal for a moment, and a sigh escaped me.
The truth behind Danny Bryant's disappearance had been revealed.
Then there was the darkness, and the secrets, that Kimihiko harbored.
No doubt Mistress Siesta would go on to confront these issues.

"I wonder who he actually is," I murmured to Mistress Siesta, who was asleep on the bed.

Boy K.: Kimihiko Kimizuka. Up until now, the version of him in her journal hadn't been much different from the one I knew.

To put it nicely, he was cool. To put it less nicely, he was blunt. He did have a sense of humor, though, and he was kind and compassionate when it really mattered. He seemed unapproachable at first, but when you talked to him, he was unexpectedly interesting. He was constantly trying to put on a good front, but sometimes he did really dumb things, and that was rather cute.

Each of us felt that we might be the only one who really understood him in the whole world.

We were *made* to feel that way.

"But by whom?"

Suddenly, although I couldn't say why, I felt just a tiny bit afraid of Boy K. Even though I'm only an artificial intelligence. How funny.

"Still, Mistress Siesta picked up on his peculiarity."

At this point, she alone had registered the fact that Kimihiko was—intentionally or unconsciously—wearing a mask.

He took his emotions and what he really felt, along with his goals and his wishes, shut them all up in a box, and then chained it shut. At first glance, he seemed apathetic and emotionless, but when you got to know him, he was surprisingly funny—and yet nothing was that straight-forward with him. It was all just an act.

In that case, now that the Ace Detective had seen through him, what would her next move be?

"...My."

Wondering what would happen next, I opened the journal again—only to find that Mistress Siesta had written no more entries.

How had she dealt with Kimihiko after that?

Was the current Kimihiko Kimizuka still Boy K., still wearing that mask?

I flipped through the journal, searching for answers, but found only blank pages. Mistress Siesta's entries never resumed.

Could it be a sign? Was she telling me to stop prying into her private life?

Still, there was no doubt that their story had continued through those blank days.

"Isn't that right, Kimihiko?" I asked him, even though he wasn't here.

Come now, tell me.

What sort of dazzling adventure did you and Mistress Siesta have next?

Chapter 4

◆ **May 3 Kimihiko Kimizuka**

When I opened my eyes that morning, I saw an unfamiliar ceiling.

...Which isn't to say I'd collapsed at some point and ended up in the hospital.

"Oh, right. I spent the night here."

This was Sun House, the children's home that looked like a church. Jekyll, the old man in a wheelchair who was in charge of the place, had arranged for me to stay the night.

I'd been given a private room. When I got out of bed, my head felt sort of hazy. I was pretty sure I'd gotten enough sleep, but I still felt tired.

It was probably because of the dream I'd been having—about a house on fire. Inside, a child was wailing.

The fire truck wasn't there yet. I'd just happened to be passing by, and like the other onlookers, I stood there helplessly.

"Okay, well, I'll be right back."

Only one person in that crowd chose to take action. Just that man. He dumped a bucket of water over his head, then headed into the blazing house.

"Ha-ha. Can't keep that kid waiting, can I?"

I'd probably tried to stop him, but I didn't really remember. It was all a dream, after all.

But Danny had definitely smiled. He'd started toward the fiery vortex, all alone.

I'd reached for him as he walked away, but it was too late.

"Just a nightmare."

Right as I finished reviewing that painful dream, the phone rang. I checked the name on the display, drew a deep breath, then pressed the TALK button.

"Good morning. Did you manage to sleep without me there?" said a voice I didn't recognize.

The name displayed hadn't been wrong, though.

"Yeah, I was fine. I was just thinking I missed your snores, Gekka."

"I don't snore, all right? ...I don't think," she muttered. She sounded cross, but not quite sure of herself. "I swear. And here I was worried about you."

It seems I'd been on her mind because of what had happened yesterday.

After our visit, Gekka had said she had work to do and went back to the hotel by herself. So I was the only one who'd stayed at Sun House last night, and apparently, she'd been worried enough to call me.

"That's very kind of you," I said diplomatically.

"Well, I am an adult," she responded, sounding like a kid.

She might not actually be that much older than me after all.

"What?"

"Nothing."

Still, what made Gekka want to change up her appearance every time? She seemed to be using a voice changer again today; her voice had been different yesterday. She must have wanted to conceal her identity at all costs.

Was that her work style, or was it the policy of the organization that sent her on missions? Either way, she was probably still hiding a lot from me.

At this point, though, I wasn't planning to get to the bottom of it. Assuming it wasn't related to Danny's death, anyway.

"Well, Gekka-the-adult? What are you cosplaying as today?" Switching gears, I started joking around with her.

"I just got out of the shower, so I'm naked. Stark naked."

"Put on some clothes before you use the phone."

That's no good. Even if she was actually an adult, she was a hopeless one.

"Kid, what sort of cosplays do you like?"

It's way too early in the day for this sort of conversation.

"If we don't discuss what I'll be wearing, you won't recognize me the next time we meet, remember?"

Ah, I see. So we were making arrangements for next time. ...Meaning there was going to be a next time? I didn't know what business she was being called out on, but I thought about it carefully before I answered. "A nurse, or a cheerleader."

"Huh! So that's what you're int—"

"Only a layman would answer with either of those."

"A layman...," Gekka echoed, sounding mystified.

"For an expert..."

"What?"

"It's gotta be family restaurant uniforms."

"............"

Silence.

"Then uniforms from convenience stores or fast-food joints."

"............"

There seemed to be poor connection. Was it because my smartphone was two generations old?

"When did the signal cut out?"

"It didn't. I heard all of that."

"I see. Then let's move on to the main topic."

Life is short. After having a pointless conversation, you have to work faster than usual.

What was Gekka actually calling about?

"Yes, well..." She was still a little evasive. "It's important, so maybe we should meet in person. My business will be wrapped up before the end of the day."

So we really would be seeing each other again.

"Yeah, okay. Where and when do you want to meet? I was planning to head back home after this." I thought I'd done everything I needed to do at this facility. Yesterday had tired me out, so I'd rested for a night, but I meant to go home today.

"Actually, I may not be able to answer the phone for a little while. I'll call you again later."

"You sure are busy."

"Yes, because I'm Ms. Gekka."

I didn't get the connection there. We both said "See you" and hung up.

The conversation had been nothing but banter, and now the room was quiet again.

Silently, I went over what Gekka had said.

"Is it about Danny, or...?"

She'd mentioned something important. Using common sense, it would probably be him. Yesterday, after we'd split up, I'd spent some time thinking about Danny.

Really, though, I shouldn't have needed to. I'd already come to terms with the fact that Danny was dead. Meeting Gekka just made me think about him again, though, and I'd uncovered one new piece of information.

Danny had been sheltering children with special circumstances here in the Hokuriku region. It sounded like something he'd do, and I'm sure it was because of his own philosophy, not because he hoped to get anything out of it.

"Then what about me?"

He must not have thought I was somebody he needed to protect. If he had, he wouldn't have left me behind in that apartment by myself. It was just like that dream: I'd reached out with everything I had, but Danny had run into that inferno, and he'd never looked back.

"It's fine that way."

Danny wasn't my dad, and I wasn't his kid. We weren't family.

I wasn't sulking about it, and I wasn't being sarcastic.

It was just a fact. That was our relationship.

Just then, someone knocked twice.

"Come in," I said, and Grete opened the door.

"Um, w-would you like to eat breakfast with us?"

She still seemed a little embarrassed, but she smiled at me bashfully. It was as if she were welcoming me into their circle...to the family Danny Bryant had made. What was the right way to react to that? I didn't know, but I nodded. "I'll be right there."

As always, fake smiles were handy.

I hadn't expected the breakfast invitation. On top of that, it had been a long time since I sat at a table with other people, let alone a group this large.

Feeling a little bewildered, I kept working on my stew and bread. Before long, Grete sat down beside me and talked to me about this and that. More than half the conversation was about Danny. Still, the man in her memories was a little different from the one in mine.

From what she told me, Danny had brought a present for each of the kids whenever he'd visited the facility. He'd smiled and complimented them on their special skills and quirks and helped them grow, acting just like a real dad.

"...What's with that difference in treatment?" I griped at my deceased self-proclaimed teacher. No matter how far back I went, I couldn't remember him ever complimenting me. He'd certainly never given me presents. *He was the sort of guy who'd die three days before my birthday.* Geez. He could have at least paid the apartment's electricity bill before he went.

Silently grumbling about that, I finished breakfast, then headed for Jekyll's room. I was an outsider, but apparently, he had something important to tell me.

Come to think of it, when Gekka and I had come to the facility yesterday, Jekyll had looked at us and said, "I thought you'd come someday." What had that been about? Still wondering about that, I knocked on the door of the room where Jekyll was waiting.

"I'm glad you're here."

When I opened the door and walked in, the old man welcomed me from his wheelchair. The room was set up like an office, and Jekyll was in front of a bookshelf that stood against the wall. He was holding a book. "I asked you to come because I needed help to move this shelf."

Yeesh. Apparently, I'd been called in as a handyman. Hadn't he had something important to discuss with me? ...I did owe him for my room and board, though. Sighing inwardly, I headed toward the bookshelf. "Which way do you want me to move it? Left or right?"

I switched places with Jekyll in front of the shelf. There were several hundred books on it. Would I have to empty it first? Just as I'd started to wonder about that...

"Could you push it back?" Jekyll asked. He wanted me to push the shelf, not left or right, but back.

The big shelf was set right up against the wall. Pushing it back seemed pretty pointless. However—

"...Is this a ninja house?"

Just to see, I did as Jekyll had instructed, and what had looked like a bookshelf swung back like a door and beckoned me into unknown territory.

"I guess not going home yesterday was the right move."

Although I didn't know what was waiting for me there yet.

Jekyll was wearing a small smile. I made eye contact with him, then we both passed through the door. As we continued down a chilly corridor, Jekyll wheeling his chair by himself, he began to explain.

"This facility, and particularly this space, was originally a safe house for Danny Bryant. The man really was quite reckless, so he had many enemies."

Most of that wasn't news to me. Danny had spent a lot of time away from the apartment where we lived; during some of those trips, he must have been lying low here. It would have been partly in order to get away from his enemies, but he'd probably also wanted to shower the kids here with affection.

"I only know bits and pieces about the sort of work he did, and how he came to create this facility. He almost seemed to be trying to erase any traces that he'd lived at all. But..." Jekyll stopped in front of a wall.

No, what I'd thought was a wall was actually an enormous safe.

"Inside this safe is classified information about a certain job, something Danny kept hidden until his death. He gave me this message: 'Someday, children capable of opening this Pandora's box will appear.'"

Jekyll looked up at me from his wheelchair.

His gaze seemed different from the gentle one I'd seen before.

"Last year, soon after his disappearance, a sealed letter arrived at Sun House. It held strings of numbers that appeared to be a code; once we'd decoded it, we were left with a number that we believed was the key to this safe."

"...You decoded it? It was that easy to figure out?" What was the point of a cipher anyone could break?

"Yes, a quantum computer could have broken it easily, given a few years." You wouldn't think it by looking at him, but apparently, this old man cracked jokes. "However, there's a child at this facility who's *rather clever with numbers*. Thanks to him, we solved the riddle in a matter of days."

"...I guess AI and robots aren't quite ready to outshine humans."

Jekyll was probably talking about a *gifted* kid like Grete, someone with extraordinary skills. Danny must have had some sort of reason for housing those kids here.

"However, simply turning the dial didn't open the safe. You see, this enormous black box has one other small lock." Narrowing his eyes, Jekyll gazed at a little keyhole near the dial. Without that key, it wouldn't open.

"I imagine you understand what I'm getting at?" he asked, without even glancing at me.

"...This is bizarre." I couldn't even manage a self-deprecating smile. I sighed. "I wasn't his family. There's no way he'd leave something that important with me."

Who, or what, had Danny been protecting this safe from? He hadn't even told me that. Of course I didn't have the key.

"Using your emotions to determine anything is a very difficult task," Jekyll said, with his mild voice. I turned around. He was watching me with kind eyes. "People often say that life is a series of choices, but I believe that basing those choices on your own emotions is a risky endeavor. Joy, anger, and sadness can flare up inside us, but we can't sustain the intensity of the moment when they do. However, when pressed to make a significant decision, we invariably rely on those intense, fluctuating feelings. Even I still do it, at my age," he said ruefully. "In the midst of that chaotic torrent of emotions, we're subject to the passion that holds the most color in that moment. We yield to it, even though we'll already be a different person by tomorrow's first light."

What was Jekyll trying to say? What was he telling me? I didn't even have to ask. But then what should I do? If he was saying not to rely on my feelings, what should I rely on?

"—Memories, huh?"

The things that had happened to me. Objective facts that I'd actually experienced.

That's right. That's what I'd told Grete yesterday.

When your heart wavers, when you hesitate over a decision, you can rely on the memories that have been etched into you.

What had I heard from Danny, over those two years? What had he shown me? What had he entrusted to me? What on earth had he—

"I take it you've thought of something?" When Jekyll spoke, I turned to look at him, startled. He was smiling again. "I won't ask for that answer now. Just keep it deep within you, and do what you need to do."

Jekyll was encouraging me. He'd left this in my hands—the key to open this enormous Pandora's box, and the right to do it.

"Uncovering the secrets hidden at the end of a grand adventure is a mission that's always given to young people. Old soldiers can only watch over you." Jekyll sounded self-deprecating, but he blinked in a slow, satisfied way.

Then he went on: "This may sound melodramatic to you now, but that's all right. Someday, old as I am, I would like you to tell me a tale in which you turn the world upside down, forging even intense emotions into a weapon."

◆ May 3   Siesta

Yesterday, I'd left Boy K. at Sun House and spent a night at the hotel. Today I headed farther north, toward Hokkaido. I wasn't going for fun or sightseeing, of course; it was a business trip. Detectives are always expected to be light on their feet.

"Mm, yum… This is in a league of its own."

The calendar said it was early summer, but it was still chilly up here. That didn't mean I would miss out on the local delicacies. Licking a soft serve, I strode along under a clear blue sky.

I'd bought the ice cream at a popular local convenience store, and it tasted completely different from the stuff that was sold at the nationwide chain stores. All the different ice creams I'd bought here had been delicious.

"Um, not that I'm here for fun, of course."

All of a detective's actions have meaning. Once I'd finished my ice cream, I started craving something spicy, so I stopped by a ramen shop at the edge of town.

This place wasn't famous enough to appear in magazines. It seemed like a hideaway known only to a select few, and even after I'd stepped inside, I didn't see any other customers.

I ordered a miso ramen with extra corn from the meal ticket machine, then waited at the counter for three minutes. "Order up!" The manager shouted energetically, and a bowl of ramen piled high with corn and bean sprouts arrived.

The aroma whetted my appetite. I took a mouthful of the soup first— delicious. I had the feeling that was all I'd been saying for a while now, but I wasn't a food writer or anything. Exactly: I was a detective, nothing more.

I slurped the noodles, ate the corn and bean sprouts, slurped more noodles, and finished the whole bowl in five minutes. As I was wiping my mouth on a paper napkin, the manager smiled. "We can throw in some rice to round out the meal," he said.

What a luxurious offer. I responded gratefully: "In that case, make it curry rice."

The manager's expression froze for a moment. Then he asked, "How spicy?" Oh, good. *I'd gotten through.*

"A seven on that famous one-to-ten scale."

"Understood," the manager said, and withdrew into the kitchen.

That exchange was the password.

I left my chair and opened the door to the bathroom at the back of the shop, even though the sign said FOR EMPLOYEES ONLY. There was no toilet in there, just a small open space, and another door.

Without hesitating, I opened it—and this time, I found myself in a compact bar.

"Found you." The person I'd come to see was sitting at the counter. "Hello, Bruno."

The white-whiskered old gentleman lightly raised his glass to me. "Could I trouble you to put all your belongings in there?"

I realized that a man in a dark suit was standing behind me. A Man in Black. I dropped my smartphone into the basket he held out.

"I apologize for being cautious. It isn't that I don't trust you."

"No, considering your position, it's only natural. I'm happy to cooperate."

If I wanted to meet him one-on-one, this was an absolute requirement: I wasn't allowed to bring in any sort of device that could carry information. Considering his role, that was how it had to be. Bruno's Tuner position was Information Broker, and all information leaks were prohibited.

"I'm sorry to ask you to come so far north."

"No, I was lucky you were in the country at all. The world is very large," I said, and Bruno chuckled.

He was a wanderer who flew around the world, constantly accruing knowledge like a database. That was how the Information Broker lived, and the intelligence he collected was used by other Tuners as they battled global crises.

"Well, what is it? You said you had a question for me, Ace Detective," Bruno prompted, sipping his wine.

I'd contacted him yesterday, and since he'd happened to be in Japan, we'd arranged to meet.

Right now, there was just one thing I wanted to ask him. "It's about Danny Bryant."

Bruno silently tilted his glass, motioning for me to go on.

"A year ago, someone killed him. Can you tell me who it was?"

I assumed Bruno already knew Danny and was aware that he was dead. After all, he knew more about the world than anybody, even the Federation Government officials.

Still, Ice Doll would never ask the Information Broker for Danny's whereabouts. More accurately, she couldn't. Bruno Belmondo's philosophy was *to never share intelligence he held with others, except for the sake of a mission*. As someone who knew everything in the world, it was a principle he had to live by.

"Information is a weapon," Bruno said, setting his glass down. "It's more dreadful than any virus or any nuclear bomb. Those who possess it must be conscious of their responsibility, and they must handle it with the utmost care."

"I understand. It's necessary to limit the number of people who have it. I'd imagine that's why even high-ranking government officials aren't allowed to read the Oracle's sacred text."

In the past, letting one spy get their hands on a single piece of information had ruined entire nations. Human knowledge can sometimes destroy the world.

"And then there's *that capsule bomb implant of yours*, Bruno. I know why the Men in Black have the detonator."

Bruno always had the Men in Black around the world monitor his location. If an organization captured and tortured him, the Men in Black would detonate the bomb before his enemies pried anything out of him. That was how the one who shouldered the world's knowledge lived.

"You know that, *Daydream*, and you're asking me for information?" Bruno said, using my byname. He wasn't glaring at me or eyeing me with cold contempt. He simply asked me: Was I prepared to learn something, knowing that it might destabilize the world?

"Yes. I've decided this is something I need to hear, even if it means going that far." I answered without hesitation. If I hadn't been prepared, I wouldn't have been here. "I don't expect you to tell me everything, of course. I just want to know who Danny Bryant was fighting, even if you can only give me the basics."

"As the Ace Detective, I do think you'll find that answer on your own someday." Bruno narrowed his eyes, gazing up at me.

"...True. Someday. However, I think something irreversible may happen if I don't learn this right now."

Bruno shook his head. "That isn't a given. Besides, even if the situation is irreversible, global affairs are always accompanied by sacrifices. If that is what the world has chosen, sometimes we must allow it. We have no choice. Our mission is merely to fix the world's balance when it may veer too far. You understand that, don't you?" Although his voice was gentle, he lectured me sternly. Coming from him, the Tuner who'd held his position the longest, those words carried a lot of weight. This wasn't a conversation for pat answers.

We can't save all mankind. We can't prevent everyone from getting hurt. The Assassin, the Inventor, and the Vampire would all have said the same thing. I couldn't deny it, either. Doing so would have been the ultimate insult to previous guardians of the world.

I knew this, and even so... "If I learn this information now, I guarantee it will preserve the world's balance someday. Please, tell me who killed Danny Bryant." I bowed.

"You say that information will help save the world one day? What makes you think so?"

Instinctively, I knew that was his final question. Everything hung on my next answer. I needed one that would convince him.

What could I say to persuade the sum of the world's knowledge? What did I have? As a detective, as a human being, what did I—

No, that wasn't right: *What didn't I have?*

"I've never asked you for the information I most want to know." Head still bowed, I began to speak. "Even so, *I am humbling myself to you, not for my usual duties, but for the sake of a boy I just met.* The resolution I've shown in doing so is the only answer I can give."

I didn't have much.

I had nothing that would make me a match for someone who'd lived ten times as long as I had and knew everything in the world.

It was the truth, so I turned what I didn't have into my weapon.

Those lost memories of mine.

I was always searching for them; they were something I'd always wanted to know.

But I'd find those on my own someday. I would deliver my answer as a detective.

"In sharing that knowledge with me, you'll be saving that boy. Someday, he'll become the singularity who will shift the world's axis."

And so, this time. Just this once—

"There was a certain vigilante group that claimed justice was on their side," Bruno began. "They used the names of the world's currencies as code names, and I'm told they came together to defeat a great evil."

With a soft clink, he set his wineglass down on the bar.

"The name of that great evil was Danny Bryant."

◆ May 3 Kimihiko Kimizuka

After hearing about the safe Danny Bryant had left at Sun House, I headed back home. I transferred from bus to train to the bullet train, then to another train. After a ten-minute walk from the closest station, my boring old apartment came into view.

"I was planning to come back here anyway," I muttered to no one in particular.

I'd found out the truth behind those pictures Danny had taken such good care of. That alone was worth that visit to the facility. I was coming home with results, which was why I wasn't seriously hoping that the key to the safe *might be at my place.*

That was what I told myself, at any rate.

I climbed the familiar metal stairs, turned the doorknob—and there was the apartment, just as it had been when I left it.

That wasn't something I could take for granted, though. Just the other day, a sneaky, mysterious thief had broken in. The apartment's windows were reinforced glass—Danny had been oddly insistent about that—so I had no clue how the prowler had gotten in.

"...Come to think of it, that break-in happened around the time I met Gekka."

As far as damage went, nothing had been stolen. Several magazines that I'd had in the closet had been set out on the bookshelf, and that was it.

"Don't tell me that bizarre break-in was her doing."

Gekka had been after Danny at the time. It wouldn't have been strange for her to do something like that and call it a background check. Next time I saw her, I'd give her an interrogation.

With a small sigh, I headed for the closet. I didn't check it much, and when I opened the door, it smelled musty. There was a ton of junk inside. It wasn't my childhood toys or anything—just souvenirs that Danny had picked up while traveling.

In that mountain of junk, I found a *magic wishing mallet* made out of ceramic. At a glance, it was just a normal regional craft. If there was one thing that made it special, it was the fact that it had arrived in the mail a year ago, three days after Danny Bryant disappeared in the Hokuriku region.

This apartment was bursting with antiques and art objects that weren't my thing. Danny had bought all of them. That said, he hadn't accumulated all this stuff because he blew through his money, had a mania for collecting, or because he was a pushover.

For example, those oil paintings by *an unknown artist* had been the product of a job he'd performed with particular care and persistence. He'd sent this knickknack to the apartment from the place where he'd ended up dying. If I assumed it meant something, too...

"—Found it."

I'd smashed the mallet on the floor.

Among the broken ceramic shards, there was a key.

I hardly need to tell you what it was. On the other hand, I had no idea what sort of secrets this key would retrieve from that black box. Who had Danny been, anyway? Why had he been running a facility that cared for children with special abilities? Who had he fought a year ago, and who had he been running from? What sort of face had he hidden behind his mask?

All that aside, for now...

Just for now, I closed my hand tightly around the object Danny had left me. The key he'd sent to this address, right on May 5. A present for me.

"I guess I should report in first."

Taking out my smartphone with a sweaty hand, I searched for Gekka's number in my call history. I had to tell her I'd found the key... Actually, I hadn't even told her about the safe yet. As I waited, I was putting the conversation together in my mind, but she didn't answer her phone.

"...Come to think of it, she did say she wouldn't be able to use her phone for a while."

I remembered her mentioning it this morning. She'd said she'd call me when she'd finished her job.

"Way to jump the gun." I laughed at myself.

What was I hoping for? This was such a small thing. The mere possibility that Danny Bryant might have entrusted something to me was—

Just then, the phone vibrated in my hand. Thinking Gekka had finished her errand and was calling me back, I picked up on reflex.

But the caller was...

"Oh, hello? Am I speaking with Mister Kimizuka?"

Gekka didn't call me that. In which case...

"...Are you the art dealer from the other day?" I asked.

"Oh, good," she said, sounding relieved. "Yes, this is Krone. It was good to meet you."

Come to think of it, we'd exchanged contact information when we'd left the art gallery two days ago. She'd said she might have more information about Danny for me later on.

"I was wondering how your visit had gone. ...I wasn't exactly uninvolved, you know."

She was right. Krone was the one who'd connected Danny and Grete, and thanks to the information she gave us, Gekka and I were able to find Sun House. I'd learned about the work Danny had been doing, but I'd forgotten to fill her in.

I told her what we'd learned, about the safe, and the key I'd just picked up.

Since Krone had done business with Danny, I thought she might have some new information for me, but...

"So that's what it was," Krone murmured pensively. "I'm sorry. I had no idea." I could tell she was shaking her head on the other end of the line.

"I see... No, it's fine. I'm about to head over to Sun House again."

Everything would have to wait until after I'd tried using this key, and we'd uncovered Danny's final secret. Was it classified information from his job, or was it about the people he'd been fighting? Either way, I needed to know. As the one Danny had entrusted this key to, I'd see his final wish fulfilled. That was probably the last thing I'd be able to do for—

"So, Krone, I'll call you again later." Even as I said it, I was heading for the front entrance and slipping on my leather shoes.

If I left right now and hurried, I should make the last train.

Working out the shortest route to Sun House in my head, I turned the doorknob.

"You won't have to."

When I opened the door, a woman was standing there.

Krone.

"I was just about to head over there myself."

The woman's witchy rouged lips curled up.

Then everything went black.

How many hours had passed?

When I opened my eyes, all I saw was darkness.

"......gk. What's...going...?"

I didn't understand what had just happened. I was lying on a hard floor, and when I sat up, a twinge of pain ran down my back.

It was similar to the pain I experienced after having been stuffed into a small space for a long time. And why did that example have to be the first thing I thought of? Because of my trouble-magnet predisposition...

However, while I was thinking, my eyes became used to the dark. Faint moonlight shone into the room, and I recognized it.

"—Sun House."

This was the great hall. Why, though? I'd left this morning after my conversation with Jekyll about the safe. Then I'd returned home, found the key, and then...

"Dammit. Is that what this is?"

I'd just remembered the last thing I'd seen before passing out.

She'd kidnapped me and brought me back here.

"What are you after, Krone?" I asked.

A shadow writhed in the darkness. In the depths of the big room, a woman in an elegant gown stepped into the moonlight. "I apologize for being so rough," she said, gazing at me.

"...! Krone. What are *you*?" Moving unsteadily, I got to my feet.

She definitely wasn't just an art dealer. The only other thing I knew about her was that she and Danny had been business partners. At this point, I didn't even know if that was true.

"Me?" Krone said. "I'm simply *on the side of justice.*" She began pacing back and forth, high heels clicking.

"So in this day and age, allies of justice kidnap middle-schoolers? The world's going to the dogs."

"Lately, antiheroes get starring roles, too. Are movies not your thing?" she asked.

No, they're my one and only hobby.

"If you're an antihero, there had better be one heck of a villain some-where." Unless the enemy she was up against was so unspeakably cruel they made kidnapping helpless middle-schoolers seem like nothing, I wasn't buying it.

"Yes, that's right," Krone murmured, gazing into the distance. "To me, that's definitely what he was."

He. Who did she mean? Krone didn't tell me.

"Why did you kidnap me?" I tried again.

"When you don't know something, you shouldn't immediately ask someone else for the answer. People who cut corners like that are easily tricked," she responded.

…Yeah, she had a point. That was probably why she'd managed to get me this time.

But why had she kidnapped me? I couldn't possibly be the villain she meant.

Then, who did she have business with? I'd been on the phone with her right before she captured me. What had she asked me? What had I told her?

She'd wanted to know about…

"The key?"

Inevitably, I'd reached the answer. Why had she wanted it? To open the safe, of course, but did that mean she knew what was inside and wanted it?

"That's right. For the past year, I've had a vested interest in the secret Danny Bryant hid in that safe," Krone finally answered. "However, it wasn't possible to steal a safe that large, and it was rigged to explode if anyone tried to forcibly break it. All I could do was wait for the key that opened it."

Krone had said she'd visited this facility before, to buy Grete's paintings at Danny's request. Was that when she'd investigated the safe?

But she'd just said "for the past year." She might have learned about the safe on that day after Danny's death. Either way, Krone had won a certain degree of trust due to her connection with Grete, so it probably hadn't been too hard for her to infiltrate the facility.

"I waited and waited for such a long time, and then you appeared. You weren't connected to this facility, but you'd been involved with Danny. He was a cautious man; I thought there was a strong possibility that he'd left the key with someone on the outside. I was surprised when you came to visit the other day," she said, looking at me.

We'd met for the first time that day. Had that been when she'd decided to keep an eye on me? If so, had she been setting a trap when she took the risk of giving us information on Danny, and pointed us toward Sun House and the safe?

"I'd bugged the room with the safe while the old gentleman in the wheelchair was away. Thanks to that, I knew about your plans."

...I see. So she'd known I was going back to the apartment to get the key today, and she'd circled around ahead of me.

"So what the heck was in the safe?"

"I really should have been able to show it to you at this point, but..." Krone sounded rather sad.

As it turned out, however, that emotion was actually disappointment.

"The key you had was a fake."

She told me it hadn't opened the safe.

"It wouldn't even fit into the keyhole, let alone turn. I imagine it was just a dummy meant to fool any enemies who were after the safe."

Krone kept talking, but her words weren't reaching me at the moment.

I'd assumed wrong. The thought that Danny might have entrusted me with something special on my birthday had been a convenient delusion on my part.

I'd known that. I'd also known why I hadn't been summoned to Sun House, and why he'd left me all alone in that apartment. As far as he was concerned, I wasn't part of his family.

"Do you have any other ideas?"

For the first time, Krone asked me a proper question. She wanted to know where the real key was. Had she brought me along as insurance? Just in case the key was fake?

Too bad for her, though; I had no way to know. Danny hadn't left me a thing.

"What now? You don't need me anymore."

"...True. Neither you nor the children at this facility had the real key. Or rather, *that's how it appears.*" Krone resumed pacing, her heels clicking on the floor. "However, Danny Bryant must have left some hint with the children. Even if they haven't noticed it, I'm sure a memory of the key is lying dormant in their brains, somewhere in the hippocampus."

They may have been enemies, but apparently, Krone really trusted Danny.

"So what? Even if the kids do subconsciously know where the key is, how are you people going to get that information? Are you going to cut open their brains and check or something?"

Even as a joke, that was in pretty poor taste. I'd said it on purpose, to see how Krone reacted.

"Yes, that wouldn't be a bad idea." She didn't even turn a hair, and the words I'd planned to say next vanished. "Ultimately, I think we'll sail to a certain desert island. A companion of ours is there," Krone said, although I really didn't need the information. "He's a doctor who's researching the human brain. He can interfere with specific memory sectors, erasing them or drawing them out."

"......! So you're going to abduct all the children and take them there? That's crazy. You'd do something that ridiculous just to search for a memory that might not even exist?"

"We do have one more objective." Krone abruptly stopped pacing. "A certain clinical trial is being conducted on that island. Our companion is the physician in charge, and the children at this facility are special samples. I'm sure they'll make good vessels."

Vessels? What was she talking about now?

I racked my brain, but Krone only smiled thinly.

Working from what she'd said so far, I'd come up with a theory I was pretty confident in.

I had no idea what Danny had left in that safe. However, Krone wanted it, and she was putting together a huge plan in an attempt to get it.

Danny still had secrets I didn't know about. Krone knew what they were, at least. There was even more history between the two of them than I'd imagined. That meant Krone's enemy was almost certainly Danny Bryant. And he'd died a year ago. In other words—

"You're the ones who killed Danny, aren't you?"

Krone nodded quietly; her eyes still lowered. "Yes."

"......! Damn...it..."
I took a run at her. I meant to throw a punch, but the next thing I knew, I was on the floor. For a second, I thought I'd tripped over my own feet, but that probably wasn't it.
"I'm sorry. I took some precautionary measures."
Step by step, Krone came closer. Maybe she'd drugged me with something; my legs felt weak and like jelly.
"You're a tough one. You woke up faster than I expected, and really, I wouldn't have been surprised if you couldn't move at all." Krone stopped a few meters away. "You'd better thank your mother for having a sturdy baby," she murmured.
"Unfortunately, I've never even seen her."
Besides, if I'm a bit tougher than average, it's not because I was born that way. It's because of that predisposition of mine. I've gotten pulled into gang wars before, and every so often I'd run into a mugger and take some hits. Weirdly enough, I'm used to physical pain and injuries.
"Krone. Why did you guys kill Danny?" That was another gift from my predisposition: I didn't know when to quit. Since I was going to get dragged into trouble anyway, I didn't hold back and hung in there all the way to the end. That was the only way I could live.
"You're strong." Krone began walking around me. "Our relationship with Danny was an extremely simple one: pursued and pursuers. He had a secret, and circumstances called for us to take action. We fought him constantly."
Danny always used to say that someone was after him. There had probably been several someones, but I was sure Krone's group had been the biggest one. She must have hidden her identity when she made contact with Danny.
"He really was a tricky fellow," Krone reminisced. "No matter how many traps we set or how closely we cornered him, he always got away in the end."

There was a distant look in her eyes, as if she were remembering battles from long ago. Even so, I knew how their fight had ended. All she could tell me now was what had led up to the tragedy.

"All humans have weaknesses. Do you know what his was?" She was asking me what Danny had been afraid of.

What normally scares people? The idea that what they hold dear may be destroyed.

Then what do people hold dear? Their lives? Or maybe...

"His family."

The answer presented itself promptly, although it didn't feel real to me.

However, I'd seen what those emotions looked like recently. Besides, everyone knows that feeling.

"But a family? Danny didn't have—" Just as I was about to finish my sentence, it hit me.

He had. He'd definitely had a family: All the children who lived here.

"That's right. The children of this facility were Danny Bryant's one weakness. When he asked me for that favor, I was sure of it."

That favor—she had to mean when Danny had asked her to buy Grete's paintings. That request had shown her that the children of Sun House were more important to Danny than anything else. And most likely, *she'd used that knowledge to her advantage.*

"On that day, a year ago, we planted a bomb here." Krone was explaining what had happened on the other end of the line during that phone call last year. "After we'd driven Danny to the edge of a cliff, we gave him two options."

Krone put up two fingers.

"Either see his precious children killed, or die and take that secret with him."

...Oh, so that was it. Krone's group hadn't wanted to learn the secret. They'd been trying to erase the people who knew it, so that it never got out. That was why they'd forced Danny to make that extreme choice.

I already knew what he'd chosen. Not that I was happy about it. I remembered the gunshot I'd heard during our last phone call.

"...But Danny's death didn't solve your problem?"

From her obsession with that safe, it clearly hadn't.

"No, we'd miscalculated. He had died and taken the secret with him, but we learned *afterward* that he'd left a hint in that safe that would lead others to it."

"And that's why you were looking for the key?"

"Yes. If the secret itself had been in there, we could have simply blown the whole thing up. But that black box held *a map that led to the secret*. We had to retrieve that map, find the secret he'd hidden somewhere in the world, and dispose of it with our own hands. Danny really was a cautious man," she said. She narrowed her eyes, remembering her sworn enemy.

"He thought this through that far, and then he…"

On that day last year, he'd read their intentions, seen right through them, and died protecting what he'd chosen to protect.

But why? Why would Danny sacrifice his life for the children at the facility? They weren't even related…

I didn't mean to say the words aloud, but they slipped out.

"He must have seen them as a stand-in for his daughter," Krone said, lowering her voice just a little.

"What are you talking about?"

She gazed at me with pity in her eyes. "He didn't even tell you that? …He had a family of his own, ten years ago."

Then Krone began to tell me about Danny's past. Things I'd never known.

"Ten years ago, Danny Bryant lived with his wife and daughter. Life happened, and they divorced; Danny took custody of his daughter and raised her with care as a single father."

A year ago, during that last phone call, Danny had talked like he'd had family.

"Back then, he was working as a private detective of sorts. He'd take any request, from minor jobs like investigating cheating spouses to solving murder cases."

That had been true when I knew him as well. He'd called himself a jack of all trades and traveled all over Japan—all over the world—carrying out a variety of jobs.

"One day, he arrested the founder of a cult. The man was a serial murderer who slaughtered children on the pretext of exorcising demons."

That incident was way too big for a private detective to handle. That said, intuition and experience told me that Danny just might do it.

"As it turned out, however, the criminal's family owned a huge financial group. They took extralegal measures, and in the end, the law failed to punish him."

It was a common story, even though it should never happen at all. That's what happens when you're part of a privileged class.

"It would have been better if the story had ended there. But you see, the founder of that cult was very proud... Well, more like he took great stock in the teachings of his god. His god had not judged him, yet that detective had put him behind bars, if only temporarily. As far as he was concerned, the detective was the devil."

"What a load of— Wait, no, did he go after Danny?"

"No. The criminal didn't spare a glance for the devil. Instead, he felt he needed to *exorcise* the detective's daughter."

Meaning... No, he couldn't have...

"One day after work, Danny Bryant came home and discovered his daughter's corpse."

Krone told me he'd begun working to shelter disadvantaged children from around the world a year after that.

He hadn't told me any of this. Not one single thing. Not about his family, and not about his loss.

I was sure he'd been blaming himself since the day he lost his daughter, and working to save kids around the world had been his way of atoning. It was his job, and the way he lived. It had been a secret he'd kept from me and everybody else.

So, of course, he'd never told anyone about it.

And yet.

"Why do you know about Danny's past? You're an outsider." I glared at her.

Krone didn't mock me. She just quietly told me the truth.

"Because it was one of my companions who killed his daughter."

Oh, I see. That must have been how their history with each other started. These guys, Krone's group, had been behind all of it—

"Don't worry. He's no longer among the living..."

"You can stop talking now."

Mustering all the strength I could in my legs, I ran at Krone. Maybe because of the drug, I didn't have much sensation in my arms. Even so, fueled by the uncontrollable mass of emotion inside me, I raised my right arm high.

"Oh, you poor thing."

The voice came from behind me.

Krone had somehow circled around behind my back before I noticed. She put her arms around me, pulling me close, and whispered in my ear: "Danny Bryant created a false family for himself, but you weren't even part of that."

Stop it. Don't pity me.

"That's why you're crying. You have nowhere to vent that impulsive anger, and it's driving you forward."

I'm not mad, and I'm not crying!

I just want to avenge him, at least…!

"That's enough. You don't need to worry. There's something else I was supposed to tell you, but I'm sure *your heart can't take* any more. We'll put you out of your misery now. That's our duty, as those who do what's right in the world," Krone said.

The hall's big window shattered, and a figure stepped through it. They wore a hooded cloak and a monkey-like beast mask, and their right hand gripped a bloody ax.

"Behead this poor little lamb, Baht."

Was this another of Krone's friends? One of the antihero posers who'd killed Danny—

"——!"

A rush of heat swept through me. It felt as if my blood were boiling, but my body couldn't keep up with my emotions. My legs were numb, and my knees buckled under me.

"It's all right. Baht has dispatched that Fiend with Twenty Faces already. Evil has been vanquished," Krone told me.

"…Gekka?"

They'd even attacked her. Was that why my call hadn't gotten through? Because the man in the beast mask had killed her?

"Damn…it…"

Following Krone's instructions, the beast soldier was closing in, step by step. My legs wouldn't move. I didn't even have the strength left to scream *What do you mean, Gekka was evil?!* Just simple feelings and emotions wouldn't help with the situation I was in.

...What was I supposed to prioritize over emotions at times like this? I closed my eyes, maybe because I was afraid of dying, and I kept them that way as I thought.

Hadn't somebody said something to me about this once? When you're not sure, or when you've reached an impasse. When you're in a situation where emotions can't save you. What had he told me to consider? What had he told me to look at? —Yeah, I had to at least look. I had to see what was happening.

Just as I opened my eyes, wind rushed right past me.

"Who's that?!" Krone screamed.

That invisible wind closed the distance in no time and *kicked Krone across the room.*

It was the masked soldier in the cape.

Krone was moaning in pain; she'd hit the hard floor and rolled.

"Who...are you?" I asked the caped soldier.

Facing away from me, the figure removed its hood, and long hair spilled out. I'd never seen that back before, but it belonged to a woman.

She turned around, removing the beast mask, but I didn't know her. This hero had appeared out of nowhere, and I didn't recognize her face.

Even so, the words that came out of my mouth weren't "Thank you" or "Are you on my side?" but...

"You sure are beautiful."

The woman's face had been expressionless, but finally, her lips curled up into a small smile.

"Of course. I'm Ms. Gekka."

"What are you doing here?!"

On the floor a few meters away, Krone muttered, "—Baht's surprise attack failed?" Blood was trickling from the corner of her mouth. She wiped it away, slowly climbing to her feet.

"He meant to catch me off guard, but *a certain well-informed individual* had told me the enemy's location in advance," Gekka said. "By the time he reached for his weapon, I'd already secured my victory."

While she was revealing what had happened with her, she came over to me. I still hadn't managed to get up. "Sorry, kid. I know this wasn't your preferred cosplay," she joked, smiling faintly.

"Well, if you dress up as a cat-eared maid sometime, it'll work out."

"That's news to me," Gekka said. She continued, "Get back." Stepping in front of me, she faced Krone.

"...The plan's gone off course." Krone's expression was still grim, but her gaze was wandering restlessly. Had the unexpected intruder shocked her, or...?

"Don't move." Watching the enemy with something like pity, Gekka drew a pistol from inside her cloak.

"White?"

It wasn't like the handgun the redheaded policewoman sometimes showed me. I'd never seen a gun that color or shape before.

"This isn't a finished product," Gekka told me, without turning around. "I'd really prefer a longer barrel. It would be much cooler that way."

Krone took something out of her bodice, and Gekka shot her right arm.

"Ghk! Aaaah!"

The bullet grazed her shoulder, and Krone groaned in pain.

That didn't mean we'd won, though. In almost the same moment as the gunshot, there was an explosion so loud it nearly lifted me off the ground. The floor shook as if an earthquake had struck, and the hall's right wall blasted apart in an avalanche of black smoke and flames.

What Krone had grabbed right before being shot was *a detonator switch—* and flames were closing in on us from the demolished room next door. The smoke stung my eyes, and the air was so hot that my throat was burning with every breath.

"Just surrender quietly! I don't intend to kill you," Gekka said hastily. Even as she watched, the fire began to encircle Krone. However, those blazing flames also shielded her from Gekka's physical attacks.

"Do you think this is all right?"

The woman spoke from within the fire.

Her eyes reflected the leaping flames. I was far away, still sitting on the floor, but those eyes were fixed on me.

"Kimihiko Kimizuka. You're the only one who can stop Danny Bryant now."

Krone's eyes stayed on me. It was as if she didn't even see the flames around her or the barrel of Gekka's gun, and her words snuck into my heart.

"Everything I told you today was for a certain truth. The secret Danny Bryant hid was something that should never be exposed to the public eye. *Our vigilante group* fought him in order to prevent that."

"What are you...talking about?"

I still didn't know what sort of secret Danny had been hiding. I did know that having it had made Krone consider him her greatest enemy and pursue him. What on earth was it?

"Danny Bryant wasn't sheltering gifted kids and children with difficult family situations here. He didn't get their parents' consent. *He just kidnapped them.*"

"Kid, you don't need to listen to this!"

A gunshot rang out, but the wavering heat mirages threw off her aim, and the bullet went wide.

"Kimihiko Kimizuka, hadn't you noticed that Danny was abnormally obsessed with children?"

Her question brought memories to the surface. Danny was always cool and composed, but every so often, his emotions would get out of control.

It was always when a child was caught up in domestic trouble. Kids couldn't choose their parents, yet their parents were the only ones they could rely on. He'd held a deep sympathy for them, and I'd seen the sort of anger and melancholy he'd normally never shown.

"Danny Bryant's warped love for children eventually morphed into the idea that *only he could protect them.*"

Why had Danny paid so much attention to children, even total strangers, and eventually gotten attached to them? As Krone had said, it was because he'd thought of other kids as stand-ins for his murdered daughter—

"That wasn't all Danny was plotting. He also bore a grudge against the ones who'd taken his daughter from him. The people who'd just let her die. His own country. He researched the families of the prosecutor and police officers who'd been in charge of the incident and selected their children as his next victims."

"You can't mean that Danny was trying to..."

Danny had caught a murderer and incurred the man's anger. As a result, his only daughter had been killed. According to Krone, however, the one responsible had already died. That left only one target for his revenge: the country that hadn't punished the murderer appropriately. And maybe, the means he'd chosen had been—

"That's right. Danny was planning to kidnap innocent children, and that was *only the beginning*. Our vigilante group was a necessary evil. We existed in order to put an end to his scheme." Krone claimed that hounding Danny to his death a year ago had been justified. She called herself an antihero because she'd needed to be the lesser of two evils.

"Kid, you don't have to listen!" Gekka shouted again, but her words didn't even sound like human speech to me. Before I knew it, Krone's words had become the only thing I was listening to.

"This Fiend with Twenty Faces was looking for *the list of their locations* Danny left behind, somewhere in the world. That was why she made contact with you after his death. It was all to get the key that would lead her to the list."

Yeah, that's right. Gekka had mentioned that at one point. She'd said she was looking for Danny, tracing his footsteps, for the sake of a certain objective.

"The Fiend with Twenty Faces was probably trying to find children who had special abilities or skills. Depending on how they were used, they could bring in plenty of money."

A girl who could make perfect copies of world-famous masterpieces. A boy with a brain that could beat a quantum computer. There were plenty of kids like those two at this facility, and in other unknown places around the world. Had Gekka been following Danny in order to find them?

…Right, someone had hired her to track him. Her goal really had been—

"———! ———!" Gekka had turned back and was desperately saying something.

For some reason, though, her voice didn't reach my ears, let alone my heart.

She was probably lying anyway.

She hadn't even shown me her true self.

That's right: I didn't know anything about Gekka. Not her real name, or her real face, or the real reason she'd approached me. Had the Fiend's words been leading me astray this whole time?

But right now, Danny was more important.

"…! Why would Danny plot those kidnappings? Didn't he treasure kids more than anybody?"

Why would he direct his revenge at little kids who'd done nothing?

Hadn't he loved them like family, as much as he'd loved his own daughter?

"Sometimes love gets warped," Krone said. "Danny Bryant lost his beloved daughter, and he changed the way he lived because of her. In the process, love and death began to blend into one thing inside him. Maybe he lost sight of which was the end and which was the means. However, he may not have seen any contradiction in defiling precious children with his own hands.

"You've experienced something similar, haven't you?" she asked, questioning my subconscious. "You looked up to Danny as a father, yet you bore a grudge against him. You wondered why he wouldn't look at you. Why you, and only you, couldn't be part of his family. Why he died and left you. Listen, kid." Just as someone else had, some other time, Krone whispered in my ear. Even though she couldn't really have been there. "Check the inside pocket of your jacket."

Like magic, her soft voice slipped into my ears and heart. Although Krone had to be in the midst of those blazing flames, the next thing I knew, her voice had enfolded me, body and mind.

"The detonator is in there. You can use that to end all of this."

Krone was the enemy. She was evil. I knew that. It was an undeniable fact. However, Krone had caused that incident last year fully aware that she was evil, and she was still standing against us. It was all to shut down a greater evil, Danny Bryant's plan.

"The facility's children have already been evacuated. The only things that would be lost in the explosion are our three lives, and the map that would lead us to Danny's secret."

I felt something hard in my inner pocket. Had she given me a detonator switch as insurance, just in case something happened to her?

If I pressed this switch now, we'd blow up along with the safe. If that happened, the map to the secret would be gone, the ones who were trying to misuse that secret would be dead, and innocent children would probably be saved.

Of course, Krone wouldn't be able to dispose of the secret with her own hands, and someone else like Gekka might come looking for it again. There was no sense in worrying about what might happen later, though. For now, I should—

"You're okay with dying?"

"Yes. It's the duty of an antihero." Krone's illusion gently touched my hands. She was saying we should take down the enemy together.

The next thing I knew, my fingertip was on the switch.

"That man betrayed you. He didn't make you part of his family. It's frustrating, isn't it? It's sad." At the sight of my trembling fingers, tears rolled down Krone's cheeks, as if her heart ached for me.

"You couldn't be Danny Bryant's son. But there's a mission you can carry out now."

Oh, I see. Danny was gone, but I shouldn't inherit his last wish. I should make sure it never happened. I shouldn't avenge him.

The one I really needed to defeat was the ghost named Danny Bryant—

"Yes, that's the only tie you can form with him: history. Detonating this bomb will be your final rebellion against that ghost."

I'd destroy what Danny had left behind with my own hands. Justice and evil had nothing to do with it. Even if triggering this detonator was evil, being a villain didn't scare me.

I'd always been this way. I wasn't scared of becoming a murderer, or of turning the world against me. By pressing this switch, I'd destroy what that man had left behind, along with this building. Since I hadn't been part of his family, I was the only one who could do it. In that case, I'd—

"I don't understand human emotions that well."

The voice wasn't Krone's, but all of a sudden, I could hear it. Probably because of the bullet that had shattered the window. My pitch-black vision seemed to clear. When I turned, Gekka was standing there, facing me.

"So all I can give you is a hypothesis based on objective facts."

She was holding a gun. Using her free left hand, she slowly withdrew a USB drive from her cloak.

"That's...!"

Beyond Gekka, surrounded by leaping flames, Krone screamed. Her gentle embrace had been nothing more than a con artist's sweet illusion.

"That's right. This is what Danny hid in that black box." Gekka turned toward Krone. "I opened the safe on my way here."

"...You did, Gekka?" My mind still hadn't cleared completely, and I sounded delirious. How? Where had she found the real key?

"It was the key to your apartment," Gekka said casually. "Or really, it's more of a spare key. It's the one I used when I first went to visit you. I had a hunch, and when I tried it on the safe, it turned out I was right."

What did she mean, she was right? What's this about?

What was Gekka seeing? What had she noticed?

My heart was racing. Was it anxiety, or...?

"Danny Bryant was waiting for this day all along. Do you understand?" Gekka turned back to me. "One year ago, he knew death was closing in on him, and he was braced for it. He was sure someone would try to determine the truth behind his death, and that person was bound to make contact with you. He thought you'd probably be depressed after he died, but that person would help you find a reason to live again. Danny predicted all of that."

You mean...

As I made the connection internally, she said it aloud. "He rigged this Pandora's box to open when you started to look toward the future. Listen, kid..." This time, Gekka was the one who said it. "He placed a lot of trust in you. I'm not going to let you tarnish his last wish by misinterpreting it."

Paying no heed to the flames that were enveloping the room, Gekka Shirogane, the Fiend with Twenty Faces, stood tall and asked me a question.

"Do you really think Danny Bryant would have used children as tools for his revenge?"

She'd said she didn't understand human emotions, so she'd put together a hypothesis using nothing but objective facts.

We were the same. She and I were the same.

I didn't understand human emotions. I didn't have anyone to teach me about love.

There was no point in pining over things I didn't have, though. And that made me just like Gekka.

I'd been wearing a transparent mask that let me avoid seeing things I didn't want to see and avoid noticing what I didn't want to notice. It also kept everyone from realizing I was doing that.

At some point, however, a crack had formed in that mask. That was why, when I'd first met Gekka, I'd taken the fall for that man who'd wanted to see his daughter one more time. I'd wanted to know about parental love.

I'd felt that maybe doing so would help me understand Danny's true motives a little more. Maybe then I could understand the heart of a parent who was thinking of their child.

"Give me that."

Just then, beyond the blazing flames, a shadow rose up.

With a furious snarl, Krone caught Gekka off guard, shoving her to the floor. She was holding the ax Gekka had used when she pretended to be a soldier.

"—! I knew you weren't really going to burn the contents of the safe." Even though Krone had her pinned, Gekka was interrogating the other woman. "Were you just planning to have the kid and me die in the explosion?"

If I'd pressed that switch a minute ago…

"Kid!" Gekka shouted. She threw the flash drive, and it slid right up to my feet. "Listen to me! *Don't fall for con artists' honeyed words! If you're like me, then use solid facts to decide what sort of person Danny was!"* Krone tried to bring the ax down, but Gekka held her off desperately. "What did you see?! What sort of man was the Danny Bryant you knew?! What sort of jobs did you do together?!"

What had I done with him?

I remembered calling all the houses on a list. *"Ask if their kid can come over and play,"* he'd said. The people I'd called had been skeptical, of course, since I hadn't actually known their kids. Even so.

"At this point, you understand what that was about, don't you?"

Yeah, I did. Danny had been protecting the kids.

Those children had been exposed to abuse or trouble at home, and he was telling them they had an ally. He'd also made sure the parents knew someone was watching, so that they'd think twice before tormenting them further.

"Kids have a future, and their lives take priority every time."

Danny had said that, too.

Afterward, he'd headed to a home that was in trouble to save a child he'd never seen.

Kids with a future. Come to think of it, had he smiled at me as he said that? No, that didn't matter now. Even if I'd misunderstood, it didn't matter. The one sure thing, the one important thing, was the fact that Danny Bryant had put himself in danger to save children.

I was sure he'd acted that way because of his regrets. When he'd said, *"Parents are all kids have,"* he'd been reminding himself.

He'd been all his daughter had, and he hadn't kept her safe.

He'd let her die. It was his fault.

When Danny had stared into the distance every so often, he was looking at a mirror that reflected his past.

"Yeah, that's the kind of guy you were."

My father figure, my teacher—it didn't matter what I called him.

Danny Bryant regretted his past. He couldn't change how he'd lived. He loved every kid in the world as if they were his own daughter—and this time, when he'd died, he'd protected them to the end.

In that case.

"This is my real answer."

When she heard me, Krone turned, finally realizing I was holding what she was after.

But by then it was too late.

I'd thrown the flash drive into a particularly hot patch of flames.

"What did you just—!" Krone turned toward the fire, her expression a mixture of panic and despair.

"Fantastic job, kid."

Suddenly, real warmth enfolded me.

Was this what it felt like when someone hugged you? I was still too drugged to be able to move, and Gekka had scooped me up in her arms. "Embarrassed?" she asked, running toward one of the blazing room's windows.

Depending on how you looked at it, this probably did seem like a bridal carry.

Under the circumstances, though, there was no point in trying to look cool.

"Nah, not really. Besides—"

In the next moment, Gekka jumped out of the broken window, with me still in her arms.

Almost immediately, there was a huge explosion behind us, and the hall we'd just been standing in was a sea of flames.

Once we'd put more distance between ourselves and the building, we collapsed like dead men.

"...Are you okay?" Gekka asked. She was sprawled out beside me in the grass.

I told her what I'd started to say earlier.

"Yeah. Getting saved by an older woman isn't bad."

◆ May 4   ???

Late at night, a lone woman was running through a dense forest.

"......! Hff... Hff..."

The blast wave had scorched her skin, and she was covered in cuts and bruises. Even so, thanks to a certain drug, she managed to keep moving.

The drug was a powerful substance created by one of her companions, a doctor code-named "Drachma." Developed around a certain core, it greatly enhanced human physical abilities and improved their natural self-healing capacity. The drug was still in clinical trials, but she'd been taking it as part of her preparations for this mission, and it had paid off.

There was another reason the woman—Krone—couldn't stop running.

She'd just barely managed to protect the flash drive from the explosion, and she was on a mission to deliver it to a certain individual.

"......! The contents haven't been leaked yet."

Panting as she ran, Krone gripped the flash drive tightly. While her *spur-of-the-moment lie* regarding its contents had been exposed for what it was, she'd heard the password required to view the information stored inside was difficult. Even the Fiend with Twenty Faces wouldn't have had enough time to crack it.

"The secret has been kept. Now I just have to give this to..."

Nothing else mattered. Nothing even occurred to her. Krone just raced through the trees, making for the car her companions were waiting for her, in order to carry out the mission she'd been given.

"Where are you going in such a hurry?"

Out of nowhere, she heard a woman's voice. There was no way anybody would be out in this forest at this hour. As she watched warily, a crimson figure emerged from the shadow of a great tree, bathed in moonlight. Krone didn't recognize her.

"...! Who are you?" She didn't feel any particular urge to kill this person, but she held her survival knife at the ready.

"I asked first. Where are you going with that *burned lump of black*?"

"...What are you talking about?"

Krone looked at the knife in her left hand. The blade wasn't even chipped. If she slashed at the woman's throat, it was sure to produce a gout of fresh blood—

"Not that one. Your right hand."

Krone opened her clenched fist.

Something black and burned rested in her palm.

Before long, the wind eroded it into particles that sifted away and vanished.

"Wh...what?"

She'd thought she'd snatched the flash drive out of the flames, but it had already been destroyed.

"Poor thing. The drug's side effects are making you hallucinate, hm?"

The red-haired woman was saying something, but Krone wasn't able to process her words anymore. *Why am I here? What was I fighting, what do I want, and—*

"Krone. *Who ordered you to kill Danny Bryant?*"

Yes, someone had... A year ago, someone had asked her to kill Danny, and she'd accepted the job. Krone remembered that much, but she didn't have enough brainpower left to recall the client's identity.

"We should have been...the real thing."

One regret dominated Krone's mind: They would have become true heroes the day she completed this job.

"'We,' huh?" the redheaded woman muttered. Even in mid-confrontation, she lit a cigarette. "Your whole gang of evil vigilantes grew up in the underworld. Your individual situations had made each of you hate the world, and you banded together to try to change it."

Those words reminded Krone of her past.

As a young child, she'd had nothing to eat. The only way she'd been able to keep herself alive was through *theft and scams*. Even so...at some point, she'd been struck by the beauty of a piece of street art that had appeared out of nowhere on a wall in town, drawn by some anonymous artist.

What had happened after that, and who had she met? Had she resented the world once again, and banded together with like-minded comrades to try and improve it? She couldn't remember. What had happened to *the others*? Krone tipped her head back to stare up at the sky, although it accomplished nothing.

"Ruble, the man who murdered Danny Bryant's daughter, was slashed to death by a certain man's sickle five years ago. The one who carried out his sentence was the Enforcer," said the red-haired woman.

From what she was told, this "Enforcer" executed criminals who couldn't be brought to justice publicly. Krone laughed. *There's an organization like us out there.*

"Baht the mercenary lost to the Fiend with Twenty Faces... Or rather, to the Ace Detective."

So the Fiend was a member of this organization as well. Krone then realized that they weren't just similar to her group. They were a perfect replacement, an improved version.

That's it, she thought. *I wanted to become someone like that—someone with genuine strength.*

And yet...

She'd made so many mistakes she couldn't even begin to identify where she'd gone wrong.

"Are Dollar and Real safe?" Krone blurted out the names of her remaining companions.

"If they trigger a global crisis, somebody will deal with them someday," the woman said bluntly, exhaling a white puff of smoke.

"I see. And? Are you here to kill me?"

The drug seemed to be working: Krone felt as if her body had grown lighter. It might just have meant she was closer to death, but to her, that was a minor issue now.

"No, I can't kill you. Not that I wouldn't," the woman responded.

She said that was the Assassin's rule, and the difference between her and the Enforcer.

"I can't kill criminals. *I only kill innocents.*"

There were cases when global peace could be maintained only by killing the innocent. The Assassin claimed that those jobs fell onto her.

"You're a devil," Krone said, and smiled faintly.

If Krone was a necessary evil, then this woman was an absolute evil. However, that difference in their resolutions was probably what made the other woman the real thing.

"That's fine." The Assassin stubbed out her cigarette in her portable ashtray. "So, since you've committed too many crimes to count, I can't finish you off."

That was when it happened.

Krone heard an odd sound behind her. *Creeeeak, shwirr, shwirr.* When she turned, she saw another shape rise out of the darkness.

"Aren't you...?"

The occupant of the wheelchair was the elderly man who'd shown Krone around Sun House during her visit. What had his name been again?

"*Which one* do you know? I wasn't aware he was here until today," the Assassin said, as an aside, then went on. "Which of his faces did you meet? Jekyll, the kind old man who loves children? Or Hyde, who becomes a demon to protect them?"

Krone stared vacantly at *the old man, as he slowly rose from his wheelchair.* His eyes had rolled back into his head so that only their whites showed. He leveled a swordstick at her.

"Don't worry," the Assassin said.

"I doubt you'll have time to feel any pain. You're about to die at the hands of the former Master Swordsman, after all."

The Assassin had come to see the end of the job she hadn't finished a year ago. Now she turned her back, entrusting the final move to her former comrade.

Before she disappeared into the night, she asked Krone one last question. "I hear you were a scammer. How does it feel to be the one who got duped at the end?"

It was Krone's final look back over her life.

"It feels fantastic."

◆ May 5   Siesta

Two days had passed since then. Bruno Belmondo, the Information Broker, had told me about the fight with a certain vigilante group who claimed to be on the side of justice. I'd apprehended Baht the mercenary; then Boy K. and I had managed to defeat the con artist, Krone. Right now, I was still at Sun House.

In the end, the home had escaped complete destruction, and the children were all safe. Jekyll, the head of the facility, had been found unconscious in the nearby woods. He had no injuries to speak of, but he was still sleeping in one of the facility's beds. Had he been attacked by the vigilante group's remaining members? I hoped he'd recover soon.

In any case, this string of incidents had been resolved. The threat to us had disappeared for now, and the children of Sun House would probably never be targeted again.

I still had one job left to do, though. In the grassy field near Sun House, after I'd made sure there was no one around, I took a call from a certain individual.

"Good work, Siesta. I expect you're quite tired."

The caller was Ice Doll, the Federation Government official who'd asked me to look into Danny Bryant. Since I'd resolved the incident, I'd emailed her a report of what I'd found. That seemed to be why she'd called.

"If you understand that I'm tired, I wish you wouldn't call me."

I had hoped to finish the job over email. Talking to people is work. It's even worse if the other person outranks you.

"Yes, I did feel bad about that. However, it appears you've *failed to record an item*, and I wanted to confirm that." Ice Doll's tone was perfectly serious, despite her apparently playing dumb.

"Failed to record something? You wanted to know what had happened to Danny Bryant. I sent a detailed account of that." If she was going to play dumb, then I would, too.

"You did. You said that Danny Bryant had, unfortunately, met his demise a year ago. You also gave details regarding the background of the incident, along with plausible theories. I appreciated your work ethic very much. However..." Ice Doll had finally reached the reason she'd gone to the trouble of calling. "You haven't said what Danny left in the safe at the children's home."

Oh, I was right, I thought.

That said, in my report, I'd told her that the safe's contents had been a USB drive, and that it had accidentally been incinerated during my fight with Krone. It was all Boy K.'s fault for throwing it into the fire. I wasn't to blame, not at all.

"I'm sorry. I had no idea your people considered the data on that flash drive so important," I responded.

Ice Doll fell silent.

One would almost think she'd known Danny Bryant was dead

already—and what she'd really wanted was the data he'd left behind. "But of course that's not true, is it?" I asked.

"As a spy who worked directly for the Federation Government, Danny Bryant knew far too much. We were concerned that the classified information he'd taken might have been leaked, that's all," Ice Doll responded, parrying my question with sound logic.

"Then you're saying it would be terribly inconvenient if whatever was on that flash drive became public?"

"...You're very insistent, aren't you, Ace Detective?" Ice Doll's tone grew as cold as her name. "Do you suspect us of something?"

"No. Only..."

I hesitated over whether to finish that sentence.

Then I decided I needed to.

"I thought Danny Bryant might have been investigating the Akashic records, which are in the Mizoev Federation's possession. Was I overthinking it?"

Had Ice Doll *mistakenly believed* that the results of his investigation were on that flash drive? At the very least, the secret couldn't possibly be anything as tame as a list of children with special abilities. Krone had been lying to Boy K.

On the other hand, the Akashic records *were the secrets of the world itself* and must be kept from getting out at any cost. I asked Ice Doll, pointblank, whether that was why the government had gotten agitated and had sent a Tuner on this investigation.

"Ice Doll does not have the authority to answer questions about the Akashic records."

I almost wondered if the voice was synthesized.

However, it was definitely Ice Doll's. She'd just positioned herself as a third party and refused to answer, in a tone that was ice cold and inorganic.

She'd neither affirmed nor denied it. She wouldn't even listen to the question itself. Ice Doll was telling me she didn't have the right to.

In that case, who had taken that right from her? No doubt she wouldn't tell me that, either.

"Then what about this?"

As long as it wasn't about the Akashic records themselves, it should be all right. On that thought, I asked Ice Doll one more thing I badly wanted to know.

"Is there a reason you didn't mention that Danny Bryant was the previous Ace Detective?"

No one had told me. It was only a hunch. Even so, I had several reasons to believe that was the case.

First, Ice Doll had sent Fuubi and me out to search for Danny, even though it had nothing to do with our actual missions. The only conceivable excuse was that Danny had come to possess taboo information, something on the level of the Akashic records. However, I didn't think that would have been possible for a rank-and-file spy. If he'd been able to access the Akashic records, he'd probably been a Tuner.

If I assumed Danny Bryant had been the Ace Detective, several things made sense. For example, the fact that Bruno had been in Japan, *certainly not by coincidence*, and had taken my request. Could the real reason have been that the former Ace Detective had given him a message to pass on? And the final key that had opened Danny's safe: The Inventor had presented it to me as something that was handed down from *one Ace Detective to the next*. That was supporting evidence as well.

On top of that, it had been roughly a year since I was appointed Ace Detective. Who had held the post before that? Would it be so odd to think that a certain private detective who'd died a year ago had been *my predecessor*?

"It's likely that what you have in mind is true." Ice Doll's tone had returned to normal, and she implicitly acknowledged Danny Bryant's identity.

Then she explained why she hadn't told me that he was the former Ace Detective.

"I merely thought knowing the Ace Detective before you had fallen in the line of duty would have been distressing."

Ah, yes. *That struck me as a clever excuse.*

"I see. Thank you for your consideration," I said, although I wasn't actually grateful. I was good at saying things I didn't mean. "There's no need to worry, though. I won't die."

I could just as well have said I wasn't afraid to die, but I thought that might make me sound like a child whose only virtue was recklessness. So I just promised not to.

And, in order to achieve that objective, I—

"I'm about to acquire a companion."

I hardly needed to say who it was. Of course, I had no idea whether he'd let himself be yanked around at my convenience. At the very least, not now... No, not right away.

He needed time, too. I'd wait. If the time never came, then that was all right. This was my story, an adventure I'd begun. I would have preferred not to get him involved.

There was one thing I knew for sure, though: A certain deceased detective had intentionally planned for Boy K. and me to cross paths.

Danny had known that if he happened to die while holding the secret of the Akashic records, the Federation Government would never let it slide. The government was bound to dispatch a Tuner to retrieve the secrets he'd left behind—and he'd deduced they were most likely to send the next Ace Detective. He'd assumed the *new* Ace Detective would make contact with Kimihiko Kimizuka, the person in Japan he'd spent the most time looking after.

In that case, what had Danny been trying to accomplish by bringing us together? If I assumed he'd understood the truth of that dubious talent of Boy K.'s, then I had my answer. In short, it was the kid's special predisposition, what he called his "knack for getting dragged into things": the Singularity. Danny had seen that for what it was before anyone else did, and had protected Boy K. by keeping him close. Then he'd passed that mission on to me, his successor.

Danny couldn't see the future like the Oracle. He didn't know everything, like the Information Broker. I was sure he hadn't been as strong as the Vampire in a fight. Still, the Ace Detective had the brains to foresee his own death—and to read all the potential paths the world could follow from that point.

And now, I had inherited that old detective's mission. Through a vast power I shouldn't dismiss with a simple word like *coincidence*, guided by that great detective, my fate had intersected with Boy K.'s. Therefore...

"Someday, my companion and I will reach that place."

The detective was already dead.

But his last wish would never die.

I would take on that responsibility and carry it with me.

"A companion, hm?" When Ice Doll heard my declaration, she gave a little laugh.

True, when I thought it through, this might actually seem pretty childish. Still.

"Did you know? In stories about saving the world, the protagonist is always a kid."

◆ May 5   Kimihiko Kimizuka

I'd been standing at the top of that cliff on the cape for more than half an hour. I wasn't doing anything, just listening to the waves break on the rocks. Even so, to me, simply being here had meaning.

There was a white cross beside me, planted in a spot with a view out over the ocean, with lots of flowers laid out around it. It was the grave the facility's children had made for Danny. I didn't pray or anything, and I didn't talk to anyone. I just stood there, with the wind whipping around me.

Danny Bryant. Three years ago, he'd showed up out of nowhere and claimed to be a relative, then my father figure, then my teacher. I'd ended up spending two years with that enigmatic wanderer. We hadn't spent all of that time together. He'd been away from that apartment more often than not.

I'm not saying that's why, but I didn't have many memories of receiving or being given things from him. The pseudo-philosophical chats Danny usually tended to launch into hadn't convinced me completely. In the end, I didn't know whether his way of life, or the way he'd died, had really been correct. I wasn't in any position to make that call.

...But I was here anyway. What had Danny actually done, and what sort of secrets had he been hiding when he died? There was no way to know any of that now. And yet here I was, thinking about the last view he'd seen. It felt as if I didn't have a choice.

"What are you doing, kid?" a voice said behind me.

It was Gekka. I answered without turning around. "I was thinking *Is that how he smiled?*"

Among the flowers, a canvas stood near the white cross. Grete's portrait of Danny.

"We'll have to put that away before it rains."

I hadn't noticed until Gekka mentioned it, but the sky was cloudy. It could start raining at any second.

"If I said things were better this way, how would you comfort me?" I asked casually. If she'd gone to the trouble of coming out here, she'd probably at least chat with me for a while.

"If I said this was the way it had to be, it wouldn't satisfy you."

Apparently, my question had been a bit mean. When I glanced back, Gekka was staring at the ground rather awkwardly.

Right. Danny Bryant's death couldn't be undone. No matter how I tried to dress it up in words, the facts wouldn't change.

I started to apologize, but just then, she raised her eyes and met mine. "Instead, take this." Closing the distance between us, she handed me her smartphone. "The real data from that flash drive is on here. The one you threw into the flames earlier was a fake I'd brought along. There were video files on the real one," Gekka explained.

"...Is it okay for me to watch these?"

So it wasn't a map that led to Danny's secret? Even if Krone had been lying, Danny had indeed been hiding something, and he'd been on the run from his enemies. Had the contents of the safe been completely unrelated?

"Yes. Your identity makes it okay."

Gekka explained there had been several pieces of data on the flash drive, and she'd only given me some of it. Each of the video files had been meant for one of the kids at Sun House, and he'd left one for me.

I hesitated just a little, then tapped PLAY.

Danny Bryant appeared on the screen, sitting on a sofa in a room somewhere.

"Hey, it's been forever. Can you see me okay?"

It felt like a home video. In the next moment, though, the warm aura disappeared.

"I know you're expecting a sweet, emotional video letter. But ditch those expectations, stat."

...There it is, that perfect dose of irritation. This was so like him.

I wanted to tell him I wasn't expecting anything sweet or emotional from him. Too bad I couldn't.

"First, let me say this: I've got nothing to leave you, property included."

He was talking like he was ready for the end, like this video message was his final good-bye. The contents were harsh, though.

"That goes both ways: There's nothing you can do for me. The living can't do anything for the dead."

For a moment, the brutal remark made my chest constrict, but I promptly thought better of it. He was right.

We offer flowers to the dead. We talk to heaven. We tell ourselves that he or she is alive in our hearts, and we start to move on.

But... Yeah. In the end, maybe those things aren't for the dead. Maybe we do them to comfort ourselves. Because in reality, those of us who are left behind can't do anything for the dead. From here on out, I would be for Danny—

"And that's just fine."

My head had started to droop, but I lifted it up at those words.

"I did everything I needed to do. That means I'm not leaving any souvenirs you don't need, and you definitely don't need to avenge me. I got it all done. You don't need to be tied down by the gaze of the dead."

From his spot on the sofa, he looked straight at the camera. As he spoke, his voice was gentle, but also powerful.

"So, technically, I didn't need to leave this video. I bet there's someone next to you right now anyway. They'll probably even teach you how to live from here on out. I have some memory space left, though, so...lemme just tell you a couple of things."

Then Danny began to deliver his last words.

"—Not having family is nothing special.

"Not having friends is nothing special.

"Living by yourself is nothing special.

"Listen. Don't let those things define you.

"Don't even tack them onto the end of your profile.

"If somebody asks you about it someday, and you remember it like, 'Oh, yeah, come to think of it...' That's what I want for you.

"Right, so there's just one thing that's important:

"Who are you?"

As Danny said that question was key, his voice grew more intense.

"Ask yourself that. Keep on asking.

"What do you want to do? What do you wish for?

"What can you do to make that wish happen, and what can you afford to lose?

"Hey, Kimihiko.

"What do you want to do tomorrow?"

With that final question, Danny Bryant smiled.

It was definitely the same smile as the one in his portrait.

"You're saying that today?" I muttered at the dark screen.

It was May 5. My fourteenth birthday.

"That's a terrible coincidence."

I knew it wasn't, but that was all I could say.

I gave the smartphone back to Gekka, then looked up at the cloudy sky. The next thing I knew, a fine rain had begun to fall.

"He really did get it all done, and then he died satisfied." I went closer to the cliff's edge and looked down at the heaving ocean. "Still. He lost his only daughter, started working to protect unfortunate kids instead, and died protecting them—was that really okay? I mean, yeah, he's probably satisfied. I doubt he regrets dying. Maybe he carried out his mission, made sure justice was done, and died happy."

But.

I gritted my teeth so hard I could hear them grinding. The rain was falling faster. Wishing it would wash everything away, I clenched my fists.

"Then at the very least, somebody who isn't him should be sad about his death, right?! If he doesn't regret it, then I'll regret it for him! I mean, it's true, isn't it? This is just way too... An ending like this is just—"

What words could express this feeling?

This agony, the way the world refused to go my way, this overpowering sense of helplessness.

The dead don't come back to life.

There's nothing the people left behind can do.

Even so, this emotion was inexorable, a muddy torrent that was threatening to drag me under. If I was going to condense it into one word, just one, it would be—

"Unfair…!"

That clichéd word was the answer I forced up from the pit of my stomach.

Raindrops struck my cheeks, my shoulders, and the ground.

Cold reality ran me through like a sword.

"—Are you stupid, kid?"

Just then.

Mingling with the sound of the rain, very faintly, I thought I'd heard the sort of words that would overturn that reality.

"He won't die. He won't. Danny Bryant isn't dead."

It was Gekka.

Behind me, she spoke quietly, but there was a definite passion to her voice.

"As long as there's someone who's inherited his last wish, he'll…*we'll* never die. Listen, kid," she said. "How will you live? Now that his last wish is yours, what will you do with it now?"

When Danny Bryant had lost his daughter, he'd chosen to protect kids around the world. What about me? Now that I'd lost my teacher, how would I live?

"I'm… I can't live the way he did; I know that much. I don't have the sort of power that could save everyone."

In that case, what should I do?

I didn't even understand myself, and I was still stubbornly chasing my master's shadow.

"Nobody knows what their genuine self is like. The real you might actually be a friendly, smiley kid."

I remembered Danny had said that to me at some point.

It was true: I didn't know anything about myself.

In that case, should I do what you said and try to joke around and smile a little?

How long would I be able to hang on to that easygoing attitude when trouble always found me like a magnet?

"Given your little predisposition there, if you're going to take on the cops and detectives, you're gonna have to be either a con man or a phantom thief."

Yeah, he'd said that, too.

From this point on, I was sure I'd have to deal with more than just cops and detectives.

I'd probably run into gangsters and spies, sickening criminals, and great evils I couldn't even begin to imagine. How should I live a life like that?

"Don't worry. Whenever you're driven by necessity, you'll meet the people you need to meet. That's true now and forever."

So in the end, I should just rely on other people?

...No, that couldn't be it. The time when I'm "driven by necessity" would probably come after I'd already done my best. No matter what sort of trouble I ran into, even if someone was right there with me when it happened, I'd have to keep doing what needed to be done until then.

That's right. This was the only way left for me to live. As I kept getting pulled into all these incidents, I'd end up shouldering people's anger or sadness or pain with them. I'd see how it played out from a front row seat. In that case...

"I'll at least reach out and help the people I can see. That's the kind of person I'll be."

Still chasing my teacher's shadow, I announced to Gekka how I would live with this predisposition.

"I see. That's good to hear." Smiling just a little, Gekka turned to leave.

"You're going?"

I didn't ask her where. I vaguely understood that she wasn't just leaving Sun House. She was exiting from my life.

"Yes, my next job is waiting." Gekka spoke with her back still to me, in a tone that betrayed none of her emotions.

I wasn't ready to say good-bye, and I found myself asking her, "Do you think we'll meet again someday?"

Even if we didn't arrange it, maybe we'd be walking down a street somewhere and run into each other by chance. It wasn't impossible, was it?

"I really can't say. It's a big world." Gekka didn't look at me, but I thought I heard a little smile in her voice. "Still, no matter how big the world is, thoughts inevitably intersect someday, somewhere. If you and I inherited the same last wish from the same person, then one of these days, just maybe…"

That sounded like she was hinting at something. Then she started to walk away.

"Gekka!" I called after the Fiend with Twenty Faces, just one more time. "I'll return this favor someday."

Saying "thank you" was too embarrassing, so I left it vague.

Instead…

"Just like you saved me, one of these days, I'll smash that mask of yours."

Did she think I hadn't noticed?

Was she planning to walk off alone, acting all mature?

"You're like me. You don't show other people who you really are. You don't let yourself."

She was holding herself back, playing the part of "Gekka Shirogane" behind a false face.

Her "Fiend with Twenty Faces" mask wasn't the only one she was wearing. What Gekka had always kept hidden was the thick armor she wore over her heart.

"Wait just a little longer."

Someday I'll break that mask, that armor.

So, until then, this is good-bye.

Gekka gave the biggest sigh I'd heard since we met. Then, turning back, she gave me one last smile.

"You've got a lot of nerve for a kid."

A certain boy's tale 3

"Those are the memories I have of my birthdays."

I'd finally wrapped up my old story about a certain guy. About how, five years ago, death had separated Danny Bryant and me. And how, four years ago, I'd learned the truth behind his death.

Both of those things had happened on my birthday.

After they'd heard everything, Natsunagi, Saikawa, and Charlie were quiet.

"Sorry. I know it's not a very interesting story."

I thought of those old memories every year, when that day came around, but I'd never told anyone about them. I hadn't needed to.

Even if I didn't, it wasn't as if I'd forget. I couldn't forget.

Danny's voice still lingered in my ears. The eyes of the dead were always watching me, a breath away. ...Not that it was scary or anything.

It was just that on May 5, I remembered Danny Bryant's words—the thoughts he left with me.

But that didn't mean this was a tragedy, far from it.

I got past his death, learned his last wish, and turned my focus toward the future.

As a result, this was really the story of how I—Kimihiko Kimizuka— came to be.

It wasn't a sad story. At least, I didn't think it was. Yet...

"Why... Why?" In the silence, Saikawa was the first one to speak. "Why don't you ever tell us these things, Kimizuka?!"

Maybe it's rude to say I wouldn't have expected it, but I wouldn't have: Saikawa was crying.

"That's not it! I'm angry!" She thumped the table and stood up, force-fully filing her complaint.

I'd heard of tears of joy, but apparently, it was possible to cry with anger, too. If I told the idol that and joked around a little, would she be nice and stop crying?

"Tell us more of these stories, please. Don't just banter all the time. Tell us more, more... And don't say we didn't ask you. That's no excuse." Saikawa gave me a resentful look.

Saikawa had lived worrying about family twice as much as the average person—she might have sympathized, and maybe she'd wanted to share these memories with me as well.

"Sorry, Saikawa."

She was wiping away her tears with her hands. I winced a little with guilt. "But listen, Saikawa. From my perspective, that wasn't a special story."

Danny had told me as much, way back when.

Not having a family, not having friends.

My background, how I grew up, and even losing him.

He'd told me none of that was anything special.

He'd said I didn't even need to tack it onto the end of my profile.

Because he'd said that to me, because I'd promised, I—

"...I still wish you'd told us sooner." Saikawa lowered her head, speaking in a small voice as she resumed her seat.

With a small smile, Natsunagi gently stroked her hair.

"You really are dumb." Charlie looked away, snubbing me.

Of this group, she was the one I'd known the longest, but I'd never told her about my past, either. I wasn't the only one who hadn't shared much about themselves, though.

"You never tell anyone about stuff, either, Charlie." Right. For example: "Your parents'..."

"Now's not the time for that story." The agent shut me down before I could finish. The wind blew, and her blond hair hid her profile.

Yeah, I know.

We'd still only taken the first step toward making a change.

For Natsunagi, the past. For Saikawa, her parents. For Charlie, her mission, and for me—the dead. We'd all overcome the spells that bound us and started to move on. At this point, none of us had managed to fulfill the wishes that lay beyond that in the truest sense. Not yet.

And so we'd start now. We were still just getting started.

"Ms. Gekka, hm?" Natsunagi murmured the name quietly.

Gekka Shirogane.

More than four years ago, I'd spent a week working with the self-styled Fiend with Twenty Faces.

Because she'd been there, I'd discovered the truth behind Danny Bryant's death and received the last present he'd left for me.

Where was she now, and what was she doing?

"No, it couldn't be..." Natsunagi seemed to have an idea, but then she shook her head. "Well, anyway. You've met all sorts of people, huh, Kimizuka."

"Yeah. Not by coincidence."

When I used that word, for a moment, Natsunagi's eyes widened. Then she smiled.

Danny had said something else once.

He'd said I'd meet the people I needed to meet. He'd told me that was how I was wired.

My encounter with him probably hadn't been an exception.

Seven years ago, a guy who called himself my teacher had come to a police station to pick me up.

A year after he'd died, I'd met the Fiend with Twenty Faces.

Soon after that, the white-haired Ace Detective had taken me along on her journey around the world.

A year after her death, in a classroom after school, a girl in my grade had woken me up.

I was sure all of it had been inevitable for me.

"But that's not just true of you, Kimizuka. It works that way for all of us." Natsunagi gazed at me, then Saikawa, then Charlie. "We keep meeting people, forming a chain of intentions, wishes, and names as we go through life. It's always been like that, and it always will be."

Siesta, Alicia, and Hel. Nagisa Natsunagi had accepted their last wishes, her pulse had raced, and now here she was. As she looked up at the sky, her eyes were filled with dauntless determination.

"Yeah, you've got that right." I looked up at the sky with her.

That was where it had all started.

Long ago, my dazzling adventure had begun in that blue sky, at ten thousand meters.

If you wanted to fly, however, you had to have a runway. You needed enough room to build speed. Someone had given me the push I needed, and her last smile rose to the surface of my mind.

Four and a half years ago, on the day I'd parted with Gekka Shirogane, there was one thing I'd forgotten to ask her.

Two days before that, over the phone, Gekka had said she had something important to tell me. She'd wanted to meet and discuss it in person. But right after that, I'd gotten kidnapped by Krone and ended up in mortal danger. That incident had distracted us, and Gekka and I had lost our chance to have that important conversation.

What had she been planning to tell me?

What had she meant to say, before she chose to leave instead?

The faceless, nameless Fiend. She'd never shown me her true face, and when I asked if we'd see each other again, she hadn't given me a clear answer.

I'd promised to break her mask, but I still hadn't done it. It had been more than four years, and I hadn't even managed to see her again.

…No, I doubt I would have recognized her even if we had met. Her face, her voice, her figure, and what she'd told me about herself had all been fake. We might have passed each other on the street, and I never would have known it was her.

We did have that password, though.

It might have been different before, but at this point… Now that I was able to use those words openly with Natsunagi, I might be able to use our password to find that other girl again. I didn't have any real grounds for thinking so. But still.

"It's important to keep a promise," I murmured quietly. Natsunagi, Saikawa, and Charlie all gazed at me curiously. I shook my head. "It's nothing. …The weather's great today, huh?"

Until I meet her again, though, I'll keep traveling with this noisy group of friends. As I looked at the blue sky, no trace of the rainclouds from that day, I just had that feeling.

Prologue, four years ago

It had been about a month since the incident with Krone at Sun House. As the Ace Detective, I'd continued my investigation of Seed's organization SPES and learned that their reach had finally extended to Japan.

On that day last month, Boy K. had said that he wanted to become the type of person who'd reach out to help those in front of him. However, the area he could reach was already being eroded by an invisible poison.

His middle school was being flooded with a certain drug that was being backed by low-level SPES supporters. Back when I first had the Men in Black investigate this town, signs of that incident had already been showing.

It's time, I thought.

Boy K. and I would change the future. The phrasing may have sounded grandiose, but it was true. This wasn't an empty dream or a fairy tale.

To us, this was indisputable reality.

That was why *I was sitting here now*, waiting for something new to begin.

What's that? You're asking where "here" was?

Well—

"We are waiting for one final passenger on this flight."

As the announcement indicated, this was a plane. If all went according to schedule, *a certain incident would take place* while we were at ten thousand meters in the air. I was sitting in this window seat so that I could resolve it, as a detective.

The seat next to mine was empty.

I was waiting for the person who was supposed to sit there.

That said, we hadn't arranged to meet. Even if *he* appeared on time, he probably wouldn't notice me.

Right now, I was my true self.

I'd stripped off the mask of Gekka Shirogane and was there under my code name, Siesta.

"I wonder what you'll think when you see my real face," I murmured. It wasn't the first time I'd had that thought.

Will he think I'm beautiful?

Never mind that. As long as he showed up, nothing else mattered. I'd see him again, and then, and then—

"............"

I held my left hand down with my right.

This wasn't like me at all. My hand was trembling slightly.

Would the kid really come?

This was him, after all. Had he gotten pulled into some other incident before he could get dragged into my plan?

It was entirely possible that he wouldn't come.

Earlier, Mia had told me that he was the Singularity, the person who could change the future written in the sacred text. Due to his nature, no matter how much I wanted to meet him again or how hard I tried to become his partner, there was no telling whether it would actually happen. The Singularity couldn't be reproduced. My deductions couldn't predict his actions.

Still, I thought. Maybe I shouldn't have, but I did. If I managed to meet him, in spite of his predisposition...couldn't I call it fate? Or was I thinking like this because I'd seen too many movies and TV dramas?

"It's your fault, though," I murmured, gazing absently out the window of the grounded plane.

I'd originally decided to choose Boy K. as my partner simply because he was the Singularity. When I'd snapped at Ice Doll over the phone and told her I was about to acquire a companion, that was my reasoning. He could turn the tide for all sorts of global crises, and if I had him by my side, I'd be able to pull off even bigger jobs as the Ace Detective. ...That was what I'd had in mind, anyway. However...

"It's because you saw right through me."

He'd said he'd break my mask someday.

Kimihiko Kimizuka. At first, I would have said he seemed vaguely similar to me, but we were fundamentally a little different. I'd started wanting to know how that personality of his had been formed, and as I'd worked with him, I'd found the answer. Or that's how it felt to me.

The next thing I knew, his mask had come off, and he was gazing at me steadily. Then he'd sworn he'd break my mask next time. For some reason, that had made me...well, happy. So happy that the Singularity aspect *had stopped meaning anything to me.*

And so—actually, I wasn't sure if "and so" was the right phrase to use.

Even so, today, I was going to tell him what I hadn't been able to say last time.

"Be my assistant." Deep down, I was sure I'd always wanted to say that. Not as Gekka Shirogane, not as the Fiend with Twenty Faces, but as myself.

"Even that may be selfish of me, though."

I hadn't made any companions since becoming the Ace Detective a year ago. Charlie and Mia were precious to me, of course. There was no mistake about that. However, I hadn't wanted to bind them with the word *companions* and drag them into the reckless things I did. They were both important to me, but I did my best to keep a certain distance between us.

When it came to the kid, though, I doubted that would work. While he was traveling with me, the chances were high that I'd end up dragging him into a whole lot of danger. Would he really go along with that adventure of mine, and was it okay to let him do it?

It wasn't the first time that question had raced around in my mind. But through all my contemplations, the answer had never presented itself. All I'd come up with was a compromise of sorts: I'd invite him to be my partner on this journey, and if he refused, I'd give up with grace.

"I wonder if he'll accept."

I understood it wouldn't be easy to accept an invitation like that, of course.

Hence, I'd given myself a maximum of three recruitment attempts.

"...Maybe I'll make it five."

Taking my own clumsiness into account, I decided to give myself a bit of a margin of error.

In exchange...even if he did accept, if I determined that the journey would only affect him negatively, I'd part ways with him at once. That alone was nonnegotiable.

Coming to that decision, I waited quietly. My heart was pounding in my ears, and I tried to calm it down.

"Say, kid."

What should I call you?

I got to work on the next tough question.

If he did come to me, what should I call him? "Kid"? No, that would be weird; we were actually the same age.

"Kimihiko," then? That sounded overly familiar.

"Mr. Kimizuka"? It didn't seem like something I'd say.

"I wonder if he has a code name."

If he did, it would be easier to just call him that... Now that I was thinking about it, this was surprisingly hard. Why did I have to stress out over this, of all things? I was getting increasingly annoyed.

Actually, since I hadn't seen him lately, I'd forgotten his face. What did he look like? I was pretty sure he'd had relatively normal features, but his eyes had seemed kind of spiritless and lonely, as if he'd given up on everything. That smile he flashed sometimes was a little cute, except it was only one of his masks. I was sure that last smile he'd shown me had been his real one, though.

And then, that's right—

That profile. The one that seemed specifically designed for sighing.

The relief almost made my face relax into a smile. Desperately curbing that impulse, I pretended to be asleep.

I couldn't let him figure it out.

He couldn't know Gekka was here right now.

I couldn't let him notice this feeling, even if it was making me giddy enough to dance.

With my eyes closed, listening to the sound of my own racing heart, I felt him there.

It really was him. Someone like me was here, right now, right next to me.

"Yeesh. Unfair," the boy grumbled. He was probably recalling the events that had brought him here.

The word I'd heard on that earlier occasion seemed to have become a habit for him.

In that case, I'd keep using the simplest words to cancel out all the

disasters that fell on him. I'd tell him this world, with all its unfairness, was ridiculous.

Soon after that, with all of the flight's passengers onboard, the plane closed its door and began to taxi down the runway.

We would soar upward of ten thousand meters.

Our—no, the detective and her assistant's—dazzling adventure was about to begin.

First...

When I listened carefully, I heard a voice.

"Is there a detective on the plane?"

Afterword

This is my first afterword in two years. It's been quite a while; this is nigozyu.

Thank you very much for picking up Volume 6 of *The Detective Is Already Dead*! Volume 5 brought the SPES arc to a close. However, before we start the new arc, I decided to tell the tale of Kimizuka and Siesta's actual first encounter. What did you think?

I never had much opportunity to talk about Kimizuka's personality before while having Siesta act as the narrator, which gave us a glimpse into her mind. So I think this volume ended up being rather different from the previous books. If you like the detective and her assistant even more after reading this story, nothing could make me happier.

Now then, it's been exactly two years since Volume 1 of *The Detective Is Already Dead* was released. With the support of many people, the story has become a manga and a TV anime, and merchandise has been released. Its world has expanded far beyond anything I could have imagined when I began the series. Just a little while ago, Kimizuka and Siesta existed only in my head. Now, I share them with tens of thousands of people, and we're all watching over their journey. It's a really astonishing situation, and at the same time, I'm thrilled.

Readers sometimes ask me, "Did you have this or that development in mind from the beginning? Do you know how the story's going to end already?" Frankly speaking, I haven't decided on absolutely everything, and I can't say for sure that future developments will go a certain way. The sacred text shows up in the story as a key item; it's basically equivalent to the original plot of this series, but Kimihiko Kimizuka is defined as a being who can turn it on its ear.

…Hence, I suspect Kimizuka, Siesta, and Natsunagi will keep flouting the plot their writer has in mind and continue adventuring. Characters like that make their author want to cry... All of which is to say, the story has never once gone the way the original plot said it would. So until the characters find an answer in the story that satisfies them, I want to let them keep looking for it. That's the biggest motivator I could have to keep writing.

The rest of this is words of appreciation. Now that so many more people are involved with this series, I don't have the space to thank them all individually, so please forgive me there. To everyone who is part of production, advertising, or marketing of the *The Detective Is Already Dead* franchise—including the original novels, comics, TV anime, merchandise projects, and various events—and to all the readers who've supported this series from the very beginning: Once again, let me express two years' worth of gratitude. Thank you very much, and please continue to give me your support.

Turn to the back
of the book
for a manga
special message!

I'M A LITTLE JEALOUS, REALLY.

LET'S HAVE TEA, RELAX...

...AND TALK ABOUT THE OLD DAYS.

Ah.

I FORGOT. I BAKED AN APPLE PIE.

SIESTA...

SURE.

Please enjoy the manga!

The DETECTIVE Is Already Dead

GO ON, HAVE A SEAT.

YOU'VE BEEN WORKING SO HARD ALL THIS TIME.

IT MADE ME HAPPY.

I WAS WORRIED, YOU KNOW.

YOU, WITH YOUR TOTAL LACK OF PEOPLE SKILLS...

HEY.

GACHA (CLINK)

WE'RE HERE TO ADVERTISE THE MANGA. WHY ARE YOU TAKING IT EASY?

SIESTA.

Manga: mugiko

THAT'S...

!

I'M SORRY. I WAS ABSORBED IN THIS MAGAZINE.

WHAT ARE YOU...